COCKY ROOMIE: JAKE COCKER

COCKER BROTHERS - BOOK 1 - SPECIAL EXTENDED EDITION

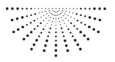

FALEENA HOPKINS

HOP HOP PRODUCTIONS INC.

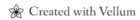

COCKY ROOMIE: JAKE COCKER

*W*HAT'S NEW ABOUT JAKE COCKER'S SPECIAL, EXTENDED EDITION? After writing 20 books in this series, I returned to where it all began. You can't change history, but you sure can become a better story-teller. So I *added scenes never before experienced* while also rewriting the entire book without changing any of the existing dialogue or story. I had some of my readers proof for typos and heard back, "I love it even more now!"

You deserved the best ride I could give you. Welcome to the Cocker family!

For those letting age get in the way of love.

The best thing to hold onto in life is each other.

— AUDREY HEPBURN

1

DREW

*W*ANTED: Roommate. Two-bdrm, one-bath in Old Fourth Ward near the Beltline. Yeah, this is the coolest neighborhood in Atlanta but no douche-bags allowed. And no hipsters pretending they're loners who are really clingy, needy, insecure fuckers, allowed. No starving-artists who think money's evil allowed. It's not evil. Stop pretending you don't want it.

Must pay your fucking bills on time.

Must fill the shoes of my younger brother.

Good luck with that. He just enlisted in the Marines and is gonna be a hero. Not many like him and I doubt you're one of the few.

If this didn't scare you off, write me, but I'm not promising anything.

I don't need a roommate. I just want one.

&

*W*ow. Okay. So *that* happened.

And I must have reread the post a thousand times, asking myself why I was so drawn to *this* listing above all others.

But did I really have to ask, after what I've been through?

The lies.

The deceit.

The complete and utter bullshit.

After the hell I've endured, this roommate ad feels like a fresh lemonade-shower on a July afternoon.

How could I pass up this blunt *honesty*? Also, I'm running out of options. Finding a roommate has proven to be much harder than I expected. I can't take another sleepless night at Bernie's.

How will I ever get a job and change my life if I'm kept up listening to loud music underscoring forced laughter past midnight seven days a week? We need sleep. It's mandatory. Especially when you're going after a dream.

Most of the Craigslist posts are fake, which is a disgusting thing to do to someone who needs a home. It took me not a short little while before I realized that their low prices and glowing images of perfectly designed interiors, are a ruse carefully constructed to lure naïve, small-town people like myself in with gorgeous photography, crazy-cheap rent, and promises of a new future in the perfect diving board of inexpensive luxury.

I'm ashamed to admit that I *almost* gave my bank account *and* social security to scammers before I saw the apartments, because that's what they asked for.

When I saw the request I was confused. *Why do they need my money now when I've not even had a look around?*

But I shrugged, *Well, if this is how they do it in Atlanta, then...*

As my index finger hovered on the 'send button,' a tiny voice inside my heart told me *not* to reveal my private financials to a sight-unseen stranger.

Thank God for instincts.

I was stunned when I never heard from them again after I explained I'd prefer to see the apartments before sending my financials. They just vanished!

Jerks.

If there is a scammer-hell, I hope they rot in it.

At least *this* post seems real.

It does not bother me that he sounds as if he might be an asshole.

Not at all.

It's refreshing he doesn't try to hide *his* assholeness

like my Edward did, so charming it took me years to realize that my own husband couldn't be trusted.

Correction: soon to be EX-husband.

Even thinking of him makes me cringe now. And not just because of what he did to me. But how I behaved during all of it, like some ostrich neck-deep asking him to shovel in more sand.

I'm not only *not* proud of how I have lived a terribly sheltered life...I *dislike* that I have. It's a tragedy to be my age, so damn gullible because everything feels so new! I should have acquired more life experience by now.

It is what it is.

I can't change the past.

But I sure as hellfire can change my future!

Hmmm...

Nice building.

Intricate crown-molding along the ceilings. Perhaps this used to be a hotel? From the brick exterior, architectural design, and decades of layered paint, I'd say this was built sometime in the 1920's. Just imagine the gorgeous gowns, jewels and long gloves that strolled through this foyer during those days long gone by.

And look at this winding staircase!

Too bad he lives on the first floor.

Oh, I love it!

Oh, I hope he likes me.

I wish these heels weren't so loud. The dark, hardwood floors are breathtaking, but they do alert someone you're coming.

Truth be told I was surprised when he responded. I'd said little in my email.

§

*H*i. I'd love to see the place. I can never replace your younger brother, but I'm very grateful to him for serving our good country. I'm responsible, and not needy. I don't know what a douche is, so I hope I'm not that. Just looking for a place I can afford because I have to get out of where I am. Please, if you've read this far, give me a shot. Thanks, Drew.

§

*T*hat's the best I could offer—say my truth and hope that it's enough. I don't know any other way. Not one that works, anyhow.

This is it.

Apartment 11.

First floor.

Oh Lordie, am I nervous!

Here goes.

Knock knock knock.

The door opens, and I nearly spit out my gum.

In an effort not to, I swallow it.

Starin' back at me is hands-down the most gorgeous man I've ever seen up close and personal. Stormy brown eyes sparkling with confusion take me in as I stare back in speechless shock.

I am not aware of it, but my mouth is wide open.

Stunned.

Flabbergasted.

Beside myself.

I am all of these.

If this is Jake Cocker, I can't live here.

He's wearing nothin' but a white towel. It's normal-sized, not one of those big bath sheets. Which means it barely covers him. Aside from that hypnotic slip of clinging cotton, his gorgeous, tanned, and chiseled-to-perfection body is on full display. To make matters so much worse, there are sweet-smelling beads of water takin' languid strolls down his pectoral muscles.

Gaping at them, I follow their happy journey down to his amazing row of ab-mountains between hips so narrow even my sweet old Nana would have imagined wrapping her legs around them. And she always claimed to have hated sex.

I bite my lip, struggling to remember my own name.

What is it again?

Dew?

Get ahold of yourself!

Reaching up with his right hand, he shakes his wet hair out, eyes locked on me as beads of water spray halo-style around his gorgeous head. "You lost or something?"

I start to sweat.

His voice is so deep that my shocked panties turn to damp ash and vanish completely.

Dammit, he just asked you something!

Speak, Drew!

Say somethin'—anythin'!

"Hello?" He cocks his head to the side. "Can I help you?"

You sure can.

As I straighten my inexpensive, white purse on my nervous shoulder, I clear the need from my throat. "Jake Cocker?"

His frown deepens. He blinks a couple times, crossing beefy arms over wet nakedness. Brutish hands fold over his biceps and I nearly faint.

"Yeah. I'm Jake."

He's not *just* confused.

He's curious.

I can tell from the way his stormy, chocolate-brown eyes swiftly travel over the white blouse my momma bought for my twenty-ninth birthday during that precious period when I'd flirted with the idea of defying Edward, and gettin' a job of my own, rather than waiting for him to give me what he'd promised.

I should've followed the pull of that inspiration. Ashamed to say I didn't, because at the time my hope was too strong and I didn't want to anger him.

But it's never too late...*is it?*

I hope not!

Jake's appraisal doesn't stop at my blouse. He pauses, then makes his way down my tan skirt and finally stops at my matching, short heels.

Suddenly I realize from his expression that I'm dressed for a job interview, conservative and proper. I must look like a boring old lady to this hunk. He can't be more than twenty-three and probably has fake tits thrust into his face all hours of the night. I must look like a Jehovah's Witness person passing pamphlets from door to door.

Oh, why didn't I borrow something of Bernie's? There isn't a thing in her closet that isn't sexy.

He says, "Oh!" as a dawning awareness brings out his smile— perfect, white teeth shining like something out of a television commercial. "You're Matt's new wife! Sorry, I figured he'd come with you for the introduction."

"Umm...Matt?"

His eyes narrow. "Landlord?"

"Oh! No, I'm not your landlord's new wife. I answered your ad for the roommate. I might be early." *I'm right on time, but the whole wearing-only-a-towel thing is throwing me.* "It looks like I interrupted your hot shower. I mean...I don't know how warm it was. I wasn't in it or anything." *Stop it! Get a hold of yourself.* "What I mean to say is that I'm sorry if I'm early. I'm Drew! Drew Charles." *He is staring at me like horses just flew out of my ears.* "We emailed each other?"

He sucks on his teeth. "Drew's a boy's name."

"Nope. Girls have it, too. Drew Barrymore?" I add as a gentle reminder.

But his ego isn't happy that I apparently pulled one over on him.

"You have two boys' names," he says with an accusing tone.

"Yes, well, I'm not a boy."

Jake's eyes drift back down my blouse again, and linger. "By how your nips turned pebble-hard when I opened the door, I can see that. Even through a padded bra, too. Impressed."

"Oh my God!" I breathe in surprise as fire shoots out the top of my head. "Jake Cocker. You're somethin' else."

"Yes, I am." He flashes a smirk that has the devil behind it, and uncrosses his arms. One of his thick hands falls a little faster and harder than it was meant to. The towel unlatches, drifting to the ground with a soft *thump*.

He is now bared to me in all his glory. I'm waiting for him to react, cover himself, apologize.

Instead, Jake flatly says, "Oops."

Keep your eyes up, Drew! Keep them up.

I am so stunned, I'm trembling.

He's staring at me with a challenge, though Lord only knows why he would do such a thing to a stranger, and to a woman.

This person is no gentleman.

"Excuse me, but what are you doin'?" My peripherals are blocked by my will to not succumb to this game he's playing. I could walk away but a stubborn knot just arrived in my stomach. "Are you darin' me to look at your penis?"

"Something wrong?" Jake asks with innocence. "Oh...did my towel fall?"

I *so* want to look.

We say nothing for a few hot moments.

It's an out and out staring contest.

My curves are tenser than a whore's in church.

I'm the first to break, stammering, "You gonna get that?"

A naughty smirk deepens and he cocks an eyebrow. "Get *this?*"

The gorgeous bastard grabs himself!

Shocked as all get out, my gaze drops despite my best efforts. He's got a good hold. His hand is not moving—it's just offering the monster to me like a waiter with a dessert tray. We have cherry cheesecake, brownie sundaes...or this cock. Which would you like this afternoon?

The mushroom-shaped tip has a couple veiny inches of length exposed behind it because his bulky hand can't even cover it the whole way. Jake Cocker is fucking enormous. Guess I should have known from his name. Damn if my heart isn't beating loud enough for both of us to hear!

Try as I might, I can't look away from the impressive offering. I've never seen anything quite that perfect. "I would appreciate it if you picked up the towel and covered yourself like a gentleman."

"I'm mostly covered now."

Still can't look up. "With your own hand, sir."

"Yep."

I yank my gaze up to meet his. I'm livid. He's stunning. But he's also such an incredible asshole I can hardly believe I haven't run off and told him where he can stick that thing.

"This is unacceptable."

"Agreed. My point exactly, *Ms. Drew Charles.*" He said my name like I'm his teacher or somethin'! "Now you know..." He dips down and swipes the towel from the floor, making no move to cover himself with it. "...why I need to live with a man."

"So, you're tellin' me you're gay. I don't have a problem with that."

His eyes cloud over. "I'm not gay."

"But you want to stroke yourself only in front of men."

"First, my hand's not moving. I'm just standing here. Second, I'm not gay."

"Have something against gays?" Two can play at this game, buddy. "You a homophobe, Jake? Because I won't live with one. I prefer men, not ignorant fools."

His eyes go sharper than German knives still in their package. "I'm not a fuckin' homophobe. I've got no problem with gay men or women. I'm just telling you I'm not one. But that's *not* why you can't live with me."

"Huh." It's driving him nuts having the table

turned like this. Who's smirking now? "You're not gay. Well, I'm surprised!"

The cocky fucker leans in just two short inches from my face, smelling better than a cinnamon roll straight out of the oven. And he's still naked. "Drew, would you like me to *show* you how not gay I am?"

My mouth goes as soft as my pussy is moist.

I swallow against a very loud, YES.

"No, Jake, I want you to show me around your apartment—that is what I want. I *want* you to treat me like a human being, and perhaps if you're feelin' kind, I'd like you to offer me some water like a good host ought to. Because I'm hot." As his eyes sparkle, I quickly add, "It's over ninety degrees out. Can you do that, Jake Cocker? Can you offer a thirsty woman a glass of water?"

He hasn't budged during my speech, still two tiny inches from my face, buck-naked and so tasty he'd break a nun's diet.

"I want a male roommate."

"Why?"

"So I can do what I'm doing now."

"Be a big fat jerk?"

The corners of his mouth tug up. "Walk around naked if I want to."

"Any other reasons, besides being a nudist?"

"And I'll be bringing women home."

"God help them."

"And I wouldn't want you to be offended."

"I'm sure I've seen fake boobs before."

"I meant by the sounds they'll make."

"The pleading with you to lose their numbers?"

He grins for a brief second, then says in the sexiest way, "No, Drew, the sounds of ecstasy they make as they scream my name."

Oh. My. Goodness.

Warmth spreads out from my tummy on a clench. But I do not miss a beat. "Will you be doing this on weeknights, too, because I will need to get some sleep. On the weekend, however, I really don't care how loud they are or who you fuck, because I will be going out on dates of my own, thank you very much."

His eyebrows twitch and the smile returns. He finally grants me serenity by wrapping the damp towel around his stunning body. As he heads in, tucking it in place, he casually calls over his shoulder, "Can I get you some water?"

Holy hell.

Look at his back.

2

DREW

*J*ake opens his fridge, producing a water-filter pitcher with the *'Britta'* logo on the side. I'm trying not to stare at his back muscles as he reaches into one of the cupboards, but I'm only human. Three sets of matching glassware placed in neat rows catch my eye. He's got taste.

"This isn't going to work...but you drove all the way out here." He hands me a full glass that's cool to the touch. "I'll go put something on."

"Don't go against your religion on my account," I mutter right before I take a sip.

He chuckles and disappears into what must be his bedroom.

His departure affords me the perfect uninvited opportunity to inspect his home. I grow incredibly curious about him as I realize this is not the furniture of some average guy in his early twenties. There's a masculine, overstuffed couch and matching chair, both charcoal grey.

A live palm brings life and color to the back right corner. An enormous flat screen is dark, with speakers tucked along the ceiling for surround-sound. Black curtains are thick and of high quality thread, hanging from iron rods. From the looks of all of this, plus the weighty dark walnut coffee table and the shaggy white rug it rests on, he must come from money, or has made his own, which is entirely possible. I don't get the feeling, from the little I've talked with Jake, that he's the lazy take-from-his-parents type.

His eyes are too sharp.

Even relaxed he looked ready for action.

Hmm...

His choice of art bears no mark of immaturity. Dynamic canvases of thick, abstract strokes in the deepest shade of every color line walls in the living room and hallway with sizes varying from massive to small triptychs.

I must admit, he's unusual.

Knowing I was meeting a potential male room-mate, I was worried I might find movie-posters, empty pizza boxes, and bad chairs, even though everything I'm seeing here now honors the photos from his ad. But I learned you can't trust those.

Oh no!

Was I supposed to take off my shoes?

At the front door are four sets of his, lined up on a black mat. Out of respect, I slip off my pumps, eyes widening at the comparison.

Fuck are his feet big!

Look at my little heels next to his work boots!

"Shoe fetish?"

I spin around to find Jake Cocker standing just outside his bedroom door in soft black sweats and no shirt. On his arm is a spidery-tat with a 'C' centered in it that I didn't notice before. I was distracted by other... larger things. Ahem.

"Yep, I'm into shoes," I smile, "Stereotypical woman. You caught me."

Jake's guard is up as he lets out an impatient breath. "Let me show you around. But I'm warning you, this ain't gonna happen."

"You're dead set against a female roomie."

"Yep."

I really love this apartment.

I want to sit on *that* couch.

For hours.

"You won't change your mind?"

"Nope."

For half a beat I stare. "We'll see about that."

Amusement jumps into his stormy eyes. "How old are you?"

"Don't you know you should never ask a woman that?"

He stretches his arms up to hook his hands behind his head, exposing the baby-soft underbelly of his biceps. Soft, brown tufts of underarm hair glisten from the shower. Or from Atlanta's humidity. Either way, it's sexy. Especially with his stomach and chest stretched for my appraisal as he repeats, "How old are you?"

"Why?"

"You look too elegant to live with a guy like me."

"Well, that's a nice way to say I'm older than you."

"No, you have an elegance to you."

Blushing, I glance down at the outfit from Marshalls. "These clothes aren't much..."

"A lady is a lady even in a potato sack. It's not something you can hide."

I blink at him, disarmed. "If you must know, *Jake Cocker,* I'm thirty-three. Almost thirty-four. And you?"

"Well, *Drew Charles,* I'm twenty-five. Almost twenty-six."

Well, *good.* That makes this easy. I will have no problem steering clear of anything romantic, because that's much too young for me. Besides, you can't get serious about a man who looks like this anyway. Too much competition for his affections, I'm sure. And I'm not the casual sex type...despite how my body is buzzing right now.

"I've seen the kitchen and livin' room. Continue the tour, please."

He doesn't move. "Why do you want to see my place?"

"Our place."

He laughs outright. "Oh, it's our place, is it?"

"It is."

"Why?"

The conversation my parents and I had when I

decided to come to this city, is still ringin' in my ears, that's why.

"Drew Adelaide Charles, you are not moving to Atlanta all on your lonesome!"

"Yes, I am, Daddy!"

Even at my age, I still called my father that. Perhaps because, as a Pastor, he is a father-figure to so many. He's daddy only to me. Or perhaps because I haven't yet had children of my own that I've not given up the childish title. It doesn't help that I'd never had a real job to speak of, no real independence.

My overly sheltered life embarrassed even me, and I was living it! So I mustered up the courage to convince my pastor father to let me follow my dream of living in a big city...away from everyone who'd ever tried and succeeded controlling me my whole life.

Taking a deep breath, I pushed on. "And it's not far. It's just over two hours away! You can come visit me any time you like."

"Drew baby, where are you gonna live? I will not have my daughter—"

"—Bernie said I could stay with her, Daddy! I won't be alone!"

Momma piped in and saved me from the look he never tired of giving me, like he was gonna preach to his congregation rather than to his only child. I always hold my breath when he does that to me. And I always let it out when Momma jumps in.

"Now John, Bernadette Lancaster is a good girl. And she's so much more worldly than our Drew is, what

with all the traveling from modelin' she's done. She knows her way around Atlanta, so Drew will be just fine! Let her go! Our little girl is thirty-three years old for cryin' out loud."

"I know that, honey."

"Well, John, I'm just sayin' — be reasonable. You can't take her back now that Edward has cast her aside."

"Thanks, Momma."

"Well, he did, Drew."

"I know, Momma."

To her credit, she hadn't forgotten that even as a child I'd always wanted to move to the big city, which in this state was Atlanta. Momma was also aware that I regretted falling in love so young and getting married right out of high school. She knew I needed to break free of the cement shoes I wore that had *Dublin, Georgia* engraved on their sides.

My parents love Bernie like she was their own daughter. She might as well have been my sister. We were attached to each other ever since we were in diapers. That is, until Bernie moved away with her glamorous modeling career. It took her everywhere I'd never been, New York City, Milan, Paris, London, Moscow. With her flaxen blonde hair, gorgeous face, and legs that could cross the Atlantic in two steps, she was in high demand and never made it to college. We'd lost touch over the years since our lives were so different.

That's an understatement.

From the letters we sent each other, it was clear

that mine was stagnant and hers traveled the speed of light. Then again, I didn't realize how that kind of unchecked velocity can impact a small town girl's mind if she doesn't have a strong support network or family to turn to for guidance and conscience. It was a big shock when I moved into her place and found out what I did.

I have to get out of there.

She keeps sayin' she doesn't need help.

I can't watch her kill herself like that any longer.

And I will not give up when I've come this far.

So I take a deep breath.

Look Jake Cocker in the eyes.

And try to avoid his beautiful chest.

"Because I can't afford to live on my own just yet, and you want a roommate. I've been to dozens of places. Some in the wrong parts of town my daddy would die if he ever visited me in. Others with land-ladies who thought dirty and uncared-for was their 'nice apartment.' And then there was the slew of lies on Craigslist that I can't bore you enough with my descriptions of how misrepresented they were! And then there's you. You, in person, are everythin' you seemed to be in your ad. If I'm right about you, what you see is what you get with Jake Cocker. It's refreshin'. And I'm tired. I just want an honest and safe place to put my head. I pay my bills. I won't be a bother. You can have as many women over here as you want as long as you're respectful of my time if I have to get up for work the next morning, when I get a job that

is. I do have some limits in terms of manners. I hope
you do, too, though I've seen little evidence of it so far
so maybe I'm barking up the wrong tree."

Oh, that was scary!

With a look I can't decipher, he's watching me. I
blink at him, become increasingly awkward and finally
cave, "I'll go. I'm sorry. I just had to try."

His voice is deeper than before as he casually interrupts my wiggling into boring heels. "Let me show you
the room you'd be living in *if you were a dude*." As he
passes me our arms brush each other. "It's this way."

Ignoring the electric shocks lighting up my skin, I
push the heels back into parallel alignment with his
boots since Jake seems to like things tidy. I try to calm
my hopeful heartbeat as I follow him, both of us bare-
foot, into an empty room that has a beautiful bay
window with loads of flower-laden bushes and trees
just outside it. This is the last unit on the first floor so I
guess I'm looking at the backyard.

My heart aches at the sight of forest green curtains
framing the view and I walk over to touch the heavy
fabric, picturing how I could decorate this room.

"So pretty," I whisper.

"Yep," he grumbles. "That's the problem."

I turn with raised eyebrows. "Sorry?"

"You're too pretty for me to live with. Boy's name
or no, you're not a guy." He shoves his hands into the
pockets of his sweats pushing them dangerously low by
accident. "It'll just cause problems."

"I'm also eight years too old for you!!"

He shrugs a little. "You're not too old for me to fuck."

Struck dumb, I stare at the dark-hardwood floor.

Where does this leave me?

Where will I go?

Nowhere.

I'll have to stay at Bernie's and get ear plugs.

Anxiety and desperation twist my insides. I'm about to trudge out of the room, give up completely. But something lights me up that I've never felt before.

I turn on the cocky sonofabitch and march up to him. "You say that like it's even an option!"

Stormy brown eyes darken as they narrow on me. "What do you mean?"

"What if I told you that sex between us is an impossibility? Could you live with me then?"

"It's not an impossibility," he smirks, tucking his thumbs into his pockets as he announces with complete confidence, "It's a probability."

"No, it really isn't."

He stares at me, loses the smirk. "And why's that?"

"Because I am not the fool-around type. And you are too young for me. If you can't keep it in your pants from your own willpower, then let me help you out. I have no desire to sleep with you!"

"That's not what your nipples are saying."

"They get like that when I'm upset!!"

We glare at each other 'til I feel heat twist in my core as I get even more riled up. He is having an unexpected effect on me because not once in my whole life have I stepped over the line in terms of manners. Here I am in his home, yet I cannot, and will not, control my temper!

"You listen up, Jake!" I give his beautiful chest a good poke and almost break my finger. "I wouldn't fuck you if you BEGGED ME TO."

He frowns, clearly not used to rejection in any way, shape, or form. "That's a lie."

"I can assure you it *is not*. Because I am meant to live here and I will be able to resist messing that up. Sleeping with you would be a *disaster!*" I inhale patience and lower my voice. "But being your roommate would be fine. I could do that. And so could you."

His eyes twitch. "You're *meant* to live here?"

"Yes. Because I love those curtains!"

"That's ridiculous."

"And that view."

He dryly shoots back, "Ha."

"And that bay window. And the cold water in the fridge. And that couch! And that winding staircase in the hallway. And those flowers out the window. And I have to start over!" My hands fly up to my face.

"Oh shit," he groans, "You're not going to cry, are you?"

"No!" I squeak, turning my back.

He walks around to pull my hands down, rolling his eyes as tears rain down my cheeks. "Hey, hey, hey. I can't take a woman crying. Stop it."

"I'm tryin'!" I squeak again, over-the-moon embarrassed, but he won't let me cover my face and now the faucet is fully on.

"Oh fuck it," I whisper through little gasps, as the pressure of all I've tried to accomplish breaks free, "I've just been through so much and I can't sleep where I am and I have to get a job and I...I mean, my daddy gave me money to start out, so I can pay rent, just not on my own! I have to find a roommate and there aren't any and I don't know who to trust! I'm from a small town. Dublin is not like Atlanta — not at all! I'm in over my head. And I can't go back! I just can't! I always wanted to live in the city. Oh, I'm so sorry. I'm being desperate and weak and...oh God. I have to go now." Tugging away from his hold I race out of the room.

"Hang on! At least let's get you a tissue." He runs and catches up with me, grabs my arm and opens a door I was just about to rush past. "Here. This is the bathroom. We'll be sharing it, but it'll be clean, so you don't have to worry about guys being messier than women. I have a maid." He rips a single tissue from a box on the counter and hands it to me. Adorably awkward, he grabs five more and offers them up. "You might need the whole box with all that snot you're building up, but this is a good start."

I half-laugh and whisper, "Shut up!" wiping away dripping mascara in the mirror.

"I'm just saying. You're a mess."

"You're so rude."

He's looking at me in the reflection as he leans against the doorframe. "Yeah."

Suddenly I become aware of what he just said. My hands drop. "Did you just say, *we'll* be sharing it?"

"About time you caught on."

"I can move in?"

He waits a beat then nods.

I blink a few times, stunned. "You're having pity on me. That's terrible."

"Please don't start crying again or I'll change my mind."

Sniffling, I whisper, "I promise I won't. When?"

"Sooner the better. Apparently you need some shut-eye. Nerves are shot." He smiles like he's looking at a lost puppy.

Without saying a word, tissues crumbled in my fingers, I turn away from the mirror, and wrap my grateful arms around him. "Thank you."

He hesitates, but hugs me back.

It's quick and polite.

Before he decides he made a mistake, I pad to the front door and step into my pumps, wanting to get out of here as quickly as humanly possible.

He follows me, body relaxed. No, that's not the right word, is it? Confident. Yes, that's the word. Which is the total opposite of me.

Rock. Meet bottom.

I glance over to the couch and picture sitting on it with a big jug of ice cream.

I used to handle the money in our house, even though Edward earned it. Numbers are something I'm good at. I'm hoping I can use that skill for something, administrative work perhaps? If only someone might overlook my lack of professional experience and give a former housewife due credit.

Sighing, I meet Jake's narrowed gaze to reassure him, "I really do pay my bills on time."

"Good."

"It's almost the first of the month and I believe that's customary to payin' rent, yes?"

His eyes dance. "Yes."

Does my lack of experience show? Why is he silently laughing at me? Ignoring it, I keep my chin up, and wipe my eyes with the crumbled tissue, adjusting my white bag as I regain my dignity. "I can prorate the days if I can move in sooner?"

"Okay."

"Well, that'll work out just fine."

"Great."

"Okay, then. I have your email."

We stare at each other a few seconds before he opens the front door for me. As I go to leave, I pause and lock eyes with him. My lips part and I frown. "Goodbye, Jake Cocker."

He frowns, too. "Goodbye, Drew Charles." His hand thrusts towards me. I stare at it a moment, then shake it as he mutters, "A woman roommate. Never would've thought it."

Backing onto the welcome mat, I stare at Jake as he shuts the door, feeling certain he is my reluctant savior —my gorgeous guardian angel who just might become my friend since he can't ever be my boyfriend.

Besides Bernie, I know nobody in Atlanta.

❧

*A*s I climb into the beat-up, old Honda Accord I rescued from Daddy's garage, I breathe normally again and a smile spreads from deep inside my stomach.

Sitting parked on a pretty, tree-lined street with finches bouncing around in neatly trimmed grass, I replay what just happened.

The newly showered, glistening and shockingly naked man challenging me to look down. The stubborn tour of an uncommon bachelor pad. The picturesque bay window.

The rejection.

His of me.

Then mine of him.

The break down.

How handsome he looked while he waited for me to figure out he'd said I could stay.

"Drew honey, you might've just done the stupidest thing of your life," I mutter, turning the ignition switch, fingers still buzzing from his touch.

3

DREW

"When is your furniture getting here?" Jake asks as I roll two suitcases into his...I mean, *our* cozy apartment.

Setting them next to the mat where I will daily be leaving my shoes first thing upon arrival, I smile and hold up one finger. "Wait here."

Hurrying out into the building's corridor, bag swinging from my shoulder, I grab an antique floor lamp that's traveled with me through a bad marriage, a painful separation, the humiliation of moving back in with overprotective parents, chasing a dream all the way to Atlanta, and finally annoyingly sleepless nights at Bernie's apartment where she endlessly entertains.

Well, not finally. It's found a new home, and me along with it. I smile and grab the base, turning to find that Jake has stuck his head out the front door to see what I'm doing.

"Oh!" I cry out, not expecting his handsome face to be there.

"That's it?!" he grunts, taking the lamp from me as though it were as light as a pen out of ink. "I've got it." He next grabs the extended handle of one of my suitcases, jogging his chin to the other. "Leave that there."

"I can bring one of them."

"Suitcase yourself."

I laugh and slip out of my sneakers, placing them meticulously beside his enormous work-boots. Walking over to the kitchen counter, I place my bag down and once again notice how clean everything is.

He chuckles the distance to my bedroom, pleased with his joke, calling back, "What about a bed, Drew?"

Yours will do.

Now Drew, stop thinking things like that! It will do you only harm.

"A mattress is being delivered later today. I'll find a frame soon."

Inside my bedroom, Jake abandons the suitcase and scans the silent, empty space. "Where do you want your lamp?"

"Anywhere. Where I put my desk will be the deciding factor."

"You're not going to have your desk out there?" He jogs his head to the wall where on the other side is the living room.

I almost tell him there's no way I'd be a nuisance of any kind after he's given me this chance, but it rings desperate in my mind, so I quietly shake my head and say instead, "In here will do. There's space. I won't need much."

He dips his chin in a simple nod and sets the lamp down by the bay window. His right bicep loosens as he drops his hand and turns around, brown eyes locking onto me like he's fully expecting to catch me checking out his butt.

My gaze stayed up, thank God.

Clearing my throat, I ask, "Do you have Tuesdays off, Jake?"

He slides his hands into his pockets, frowning suddenly. "I took a long lunch since you're moving in today. I'll be going back for a couple hours after this." His smirk tugs up one corner of his beautiful lips as he glances around what he thought would take longer. "You buy this lamp for the room? It looks good with my curtains."

Glancing over, I have to agree, and because he offered the compliment, I almost tell him the story of that lamp, but bite my tongue instead. It's best for me to keep a healthy distance from Jake.

I need this home. It's a fresh start in the city I've always dreamed of living in. To have a job and money of my own is so important to me. I will not let a man distract me this time. I've made that mistake before.

Besides, Jake is...

Oh, just stop thinking about him!

"Drew?"

"Hmm?"

"You're staring at the floor."

My eyelashes flutter up. "I forgot there's a desk I wanted to look at."

"Where?"

I don't have an answer, since I just made that up. "Why do you ask?"

"I like furniture." He crosses his arms on a shrug. "I'm down."

"You want to shop for a desk with me?"

"I told work I'd be gone for a few hours. Thought I'd be helping your movers, so I have time."

My lips curve. "Were you worried I'd mess up your home putting my furniture everywhere with you at work none the wiser?"

He laughs, "Maybe," eyes lightening up with the cutest crinkles framing them.

"And now you want to go shopping to make sure I don't buy something ugly?"

He points to the lamp. "Like this?" I gasp, and he grins, "I'm kidding. I like the lamp."

"You're very lucky. I was about to—"

"What?"

I struggle for something I might have done had he insulted my one possession other than clothing, and come up empty. "You're just lucky."

"Let's go shop for your new desk." I watch in horror as Jake swaggers up and motions for me to walk out first.

This is not how I imagined spending my first day here.

He smells too good, up this close.

I glance to the ground, and see that we're both wearing white socks.

It's adorable. I'm in so much trouble.

"Jake, I'm sorry, but I really need to do this alone."

He frowns and passes me, heading for his boots. As he steps into them and tugs, I hurry over and reach for my sneakers, the air tense between us.

Jake straightens up, untied shoelaces dangling as he grumbles, "Hey, I'm not worried you're gonna buy something ugly. I just like furniture."

While tightening my shoelaces I explain the partial reason for my refusal, "It's my personal space and if you come, I might buy things *you* want rather than what I want." Standing up I lock eyes with him to see if he's mad at me. My heart skips a beat because his smirk has the devil in it again.

Or a thousand angels.

"Why are you smiling like that, Jake Cocker?"

"Well, *Drew Charles,* because my brother Jeremy told me he hated the couch I made him buy with me, so I get what you're saying. I can be very persuasive."

I have no doubt.

"Jeremy, who joined the Marines?" He nods and I point to the living room. "That couch?"

"He wanted brown leather."

"But overstuffed is so comfy!"

"And leather can be sticky in the hot summers. You like the color?"

I'm staring at it, thinking that very soon I'll be sitting there with a jug of ice cream and fuzzy socks tucked under that throw blanket. "It's a masculine color, so I like it for you, yes." I tilt my head. "No, I like it for me, too."

His brown eyes shimmer, pleased that I approve. He points at me with an overly gruff warning in his tone, "I call shotgun for Sundays. My favorite show is on. Let's just be clear on one thing: I won't be watching girly movies just because you pay rent. Got me?"

A smile tugs. "Fine. Be that way. And you don't have to worry—I promise I won't sit there on Sundays."

"You can sit there. But I get remote rights."

"Fine."

"Good."

"Are we leaving together?"

"You first."

"You're a gentleman now?"

"I'm always a—"

"A gentleman wouldn't have dropped his towel and let it lay there on the floor."

"Oh wait. I forgot I was born in a cave and have no manners." He opens the door, mocking me with his chest puffed-out. "Stay behind me, woman!"

I hurry past him just for fun, and our bodies brush against each other. My breath suspends, and I blank completely, sneakers moving of their own accord toward the winding staircase and exit.

Jake's confident swagger remains hurried. I'm pretty sure he's checking me out as distance grows between us, because my ass feels warm.

I call out, "Goodbye Jake. Have a nice day at work."

"Bye Drew." I heard a smile in that. Was it my imagination?

I look back and see him throwing his keys in the air, shoelaces still untied as he strolls without a care in the world. Those thighs...they almost look better in jeans than they do naked. How is that possible? And I'll never forget his...

But I *did* forget my bag, my wallet, my keys!

The sunlight warms my blushing cheeks as I hurry to my Honda.

Just ask him to unlock the door, Drew.

I don't want to!

With the grace of a woman who has everything under control, I slide into the old car—grateful I didn't lock it—and casually glance over to his truck as he jumps inside. His shoelace gets caught in the door as he shuts it. He wrestles a second, swears, frees the trapped string and glances to me, wondering if I saw.

I look away in time, and successfully hide my smile with a serious expression, pretending to turn down the radio. It would be cruel to embarrass him when I'm over here hoping he doesn't know that the only way my vehicle would start is by telekinesis.

His truck drives by slowly, like he's trying to get my attention.

Oh, please keep driving, Jake.

He stops.

Dang!

Rolling down his window, he asks, "Everything okay?"

My windows are electrically controlled, and I somehow manage to keep my smile worry-free as I shout through the glass, "Fine, just fine. Just choosing a radio station. So many commercials!"

He nods, and drives away.

I give it a good five minutes before slinking out of my car and sprinting across the street, over the lawn, around the back of our apartment building in search of the backside of forest green curtains. With a few jiggles, the old lock gives way, and I climb inside the silence of my new beginning, latching beautiful bay windows once more.

As I swipe my forgotten bag from his...I mean *our*, immaculate kitchen counter, I mumble an incredulous, "I cannot focus when he's around!"

4

JAKE

"*B*est fuckin' burger in town," my brother Jason groans with ketchup dripping down his lip. No one in our family loves good food as much as Jason. Pale green eyes flicker then close as he winces, "Fuck! Mmm!"

The Vortex has easily won the unspoken-yet-very-real burger competition in Atlanta.

Hands down. Flag thrown.

Everyone go home. We have a winner.

Basking in the greatness, I nod, my mouth packed with expertly-cooked grade-A beef, BBQ sauce, fried egg, bacon and fluffy yet crispy onion rings trapped by a deliciously toasted bun. I give him a muffled, "Doesn't get any better than this!"

Jason downs his beer, looks at the empty bottle and shakes it. "Where's our waitress?"

Scanning the loud room, my gaze flies past the wheels of a motorcycle that hangs from the ceiling, a packed bar with smokers enjoying one of the last rebellious places where they can take a drag indoors, and across the faces of twenty-one-and-over locals engaged in easy-going conversations with fists full of either great food, their date's hair mid-kiss, or local craft brew. "She's probably with Justin in a closet somewhere."

He laughs while searching the controlled chaos for his twin. "You might be right."

"Might be?" I devour another juicy bite, trying to enjoy some elbow room and coming up empty.

Truth is this round, high top table isn't big enough for three guys like us, though I do approve of the height and barstools. In fact I like everything about this place from the snarky menu that tells you where to shove it if you don't like their policies, to the rock and roll, dress any way you want atmosphere.

Jason chows down some fries from Justin's abandoned plate. He's been doing that since I was born. They're older than I am, next up in line of six brothers, and some of my earliest memories include Justin swatting Jason's greedy fingers during meals. I used to watch as the thief would wait for his big moment to sneak cornbread, meatballs, even a whole steak, away from his twin's distracted vigil. It gave him great satisfaction when he was successful.

As Jason scoops ketchup with a crispy french fry and grumbles, "I need another beer and he's fucking the waitress in a closet," I cock an eyebrow, knowing there will be hell to pay.

"I said I *think* he is. I don't know that."

"C'mon. You know he's doing something with her. You saw how they were talking?" I nod. "Jake, answer me this: Why didn't God create my twin to be a good guy?"

Jason's mock-innocence and fake curiosity is highly amusing considering he's not the prince he claims to be. But I get his point.

Us Cocker Brothers are not without our flaws. However, we all know Justin is the biggest dick among us. He's had a jaded chip on his Yale-educated shoulder ever since he was a boy.

I asked him once why he was so ruthless when it came to dating. He shrugged, but I saw those ice-green eyes of his chewing on the reason, one he had no intention of ever sharing with me. It bothered me, but I didn't push the subject. That's not something guys do.

My brothers and I are all close, but we've sort of paired off, and it coincides with our ages.

The twins are the pretty much inseparable. I won't hang out with one without the other coming along. When Justin went to Yale, that was the only time they lived in different cities and it was...weird.

Jaxson and Jett are the two oldest with Jaxson first born. They're thick as twins but are just over a year apart. Both are loners, which suits them just fine, so the fact that Jaxson lives an hour north of Atlanta, and Jett's settled—if you can call it that—in Louisiana, doesn't matter. Those two can go months without speaking and nothing shifts between them.

Rock. Solid.

I'm second youngest and Jeremy is last in line.

Jeremy.

Fucking kid.

Couldn't believe it when he came home and stood in front of the television show I was watching.

"Jake, I uh..."

"What?"

"I've been thinking of how to tell you something."

I swiped the remote from the cushion next to me, and powered it off. "Go."

Silence took over our living room as he chewed his cheek. The dark brown eyes that matched my own were locked on the coffee table between us for what seemed like four years.

Impatient, I finally grunted, "Spit it out!"

"Jake, I uh..."

"Yeah, you said that already. You what? What's got you this scared? You get someone pregnant?"

"No!"

"You're gay?"

Jeremy rubbed his face.

"Okay, you're gay. So what?" I threw my arm up, ready to accept a coming-out confession. We'd both hooked up with more women than I could count, but maybe Jeremy was faking it. "It wouldn't bother me. You could start dressing as a woman and I'd still love you. But let me get back to my show! Be you, man."

"I'm not gay. I joined the Marines."

"Fuck you did!" My smile faded as he stared at me with zero humor. "You're kidding, right?"

"I enlisted. I'm headed for training in two days."

I shot off the couch like it caught fire, and paced, raking my hair with stunned fingers.

My younger brother, my roommate, my partner in crime, my wing man, my best friend in the whole world, was leaving.

I flipped around and demanded, "You enlisted? Why?" My chest tightened as I waited for an answer.

He remained silent, frowning like he didn't think I'd understand if he explained.

"You tell Mom and Dad?"

He shook his head.

"I know you didn't tell our brothers! You better not have!"

He shook his head again. "Of course I told you first, Jake. Come on."

"*Mother fucking right you better have!*" *I marched to the kitchen for a beer, just for something physical to do rather than punch something. I needed time to process what the fuck just happened. The Marines. He enlisted and there was no turning back. He was leaving, and with a gun. This was no game. Jeremy was about to become a whole different person. A man who served his country. Far away from family. Far away from me.*

He took the bottle of Orpheus I handed him before I slammed the refrigerator door.

We twisted the caps off at the same time.

Took a drink.

Stared at the floor.

Glanced to each other.

Stared back at the floor.

It hurt so bad thinking of him going. And at the same time, something bigger overtook my racing thoughts. "*You're my fuckin' hero, Jeremy.*"

He blinked up from the tile. "*What?*"

"*You've got balls the size of Georgia for pulling a stunt like this.*" *Shaking my head, I took a swig, blinking at the radicalness of his decision. I would never have expected this from him.* "*Guess I always thought of you as the baby of the family, but this...this was a man's decision.*"

His voice was quiet. "*Thanks, Jake.*"

We took another sip and stood in the kitchen, lost in our thoughts, staring into a future where we no longer lived together for the first time in our lives.

I shook my head, set my bottle down, said, "*Fuck*

this. Come here," and yanked him into a hug. "I'm gonna miss you, ya hear me?"

The emotion was welling up in him, too. "Will you help me tell Mom and Dad?"

"Hell no. That's all you."

We laughed and pulled away.

I grinned at him, seeing him through new eyes as I took a deep breath. "Of course I will. But prepare yourself. Mom is gonna cry."

Jeremy nodded, and gave his cheek a wipe, walking out of the kitchen and hoping I didn't see the tear. "I know," he muttered before he disappeared into his room.

As Jason goes for my beer, I grab it before his thieving fingers take hold. "Ah ah ah. Get your own."

"Fucker," he mutters, searching for a waitress to help us. Spotting a lanky, heavily pierced girl with dyed-black hair, he calls out, "Hey!"

She raises an eyebrow as she saunters up to ask over loud, classic rock, "You think I'm a dog or something?"

I grin, happy to discover he picked the wrong girl to ask like that. The Vortex has a thing where at least one server a shift acts like a complete asshole on purpose. It's part of the fun. They get to say whatever they want to whoever they want however they want. It's amusing as all hell—one of the reasons we love coming here.

She rakes a disgusted glance up and down his long body, something most women would never think to do. "You can only call a dog like that and have it not think you're a dick."

Jason smirks, "You're thinking about my dick already? You just got here."

She shouts to the room, "The Cocky Brothers are out on the town. Keep your girls inside, people!"

Jason and I start laughing as heads turn.

To a woman who's peeking over, I smile, "That means you," and throw her a wink.

Her eyes go wide and she flips back around to her unamused husband.

Jason asks our server as she again faces us, "How about another Monday Night Slap Fight, you charming seductress?"

It's the actual name of a beer from a local brewery, if you can believe it.

Unimpressed, she sneers from Jason to me then back to him. "This isn't my section, dimwits. Where's Tanny? And wasn't *Justin* here with you? Oh shit. Motherfucker." She storms off.

She just realized where Tanny is.

We're notorious.

Born and raised here.

Atlanta is a small town dressed as a big city. Most people know us, or know *of* us.

Kinda hard to hide when you come from old money, a long line of politicians, and there are six brothers raising hell as soon as they hit Kindergarten all the way on up. Now that I think about it, we never stopped raising hell.

Sopping up mustard with the last crispy fry, Jason

mutters, "He's gonna have to rein it in if he's going to be a Senator one day."

"Modern days. People expect less of us. Besides, he's only twenty-seven."

"And a half."

"They'll forgive him."

Jason shrugs. "When I was working with H-Core on his last album and he got caught...you know..."

"With the dude in the bathroom?"

"Yep. Fuck Justin's out of fries now, too! First beer, now this. Give me some."

"No."

Jason shoots me an irritated look, but continues, "His rep as a ladies man deflated and I lost money on that album. And so did he."

"Justin will be just fine. Don't worry about him. He always lands on his feet, like a cat."

The subject of our debate walks up with a lazy stride, running his hands through light-blonde hair. "If I'm a cat then I'm the one who ate the canary." He hits the baseball cap on his twin's head and takes a seat.

Jason and I shake our heads.

"Next time you eat our waitress will you make sure that WE have enough to eat, first?" Jason motions to their empty plates.

Justin stares at them, and hits his thieving twin. "You ate my whole fucking meal!"

"Duh!"

I raise my eyebrows at Justin that he should know

better. "That's what happens when you leave it unguarded. But I have a feeling she'll get you more."

Up walks Tanny Walters with blue-tipped fingers twined around three ice-cold bottles.

"These are on me," she smiles, eyes locked with Justin's. It's instantly clear she really likes the guy, *and* that she's in over her head. Jason and I exchange a look because she has no idea she's being obvious and that it's never gonna happen.

Not long term.

Not with Justin.

It's a fact that women tend to get their panties in a bunch over our family. Partly because we aren't a fucking bunch of pussies, and partly because of the money. And prestige.

It just makes us jaded, suspicious, and guarded, knowing the attention is fueled by a selfish motivation —to be connected to a Cocker brother means something in Atlanta.

Justin will marry a woman who will look good to voters. That's just a fact. Hell, I'll be shocked when any of us gets serious about someone, but especially him. His heart is closed to anything but politics.

However, he will *never* turn down free pussy or free beer.

He takes the latter from Tanny and uses the Southern drawl he lays on thick when charming people into doing what he wants. "Well, now isn't that sweet of you."

"Least I could do," she says, thinking she's being

mysterious. We know exactly why she bought this round. Payback for the big O he just granted her. Flashing a smile around the table, Tanny floats off, but not before glancing suggestively to him over her shoulder on her way.

He waves to her with a smirk.

"I'm going to puke," Jason mutters, low enough for just us.

"I'm right behind ya," I agree. "Shit, Justin. How long did that take you?" He shrugs and looks from his empty plate to Jason's, then to mine. I've still got a few morsels left. "Don't touch my food. I'm not kidding."

His hands go up. "Alright!" He stares at my fries.

"Stop it."

"Going to have to order some more food," he sighs, giving up. "You never answered me earlier."

I remember the question. "You took off before I had the chance to. You think with your dick. It's like having dinner with a gnat, that's your attention span."

"Only when there's a woman around who touches my leg like she did. Door was open. You would have walked through it."

I shrug. Tanny's not my type. She's not his, either. He'll get married to someone who looks good to voters. But that wouldn't stop him from giving her a temporary tongue-to-pussy-lashing if there's a private place to do it.

"So, I'll ask you again. How's your female roomie situation *coming* along?"

Shaking my head at his emphasis on the word

coming, I sip fresh, cold beer before I set it down to answer, "She keeps to herself. Paid me a deposit and first month, plus prorated the extra days."

My mind travels back to this morning when Drew came out of the bathroom with a towel around her head and body, and saw me waiting my turn.

"Oh, were you waitin' long?" she asked with that slow and sexy Georgia drawl.

"Nah, just made coffee and came over."

She tucked loose wet strands under the towel-turban and smiled shyly at me. "I thought you got ready for work later than this."

"Have to go in early today." At her apologetic expression, I cut her off. "Don't worry about it. I'm not late."

"Oh," she glanced to my bare chest.

"I like your outfit," I smirked.

"Your tailor made it for me," she dryly threw back.

"Ha."

"Well, have a good day."

She headed to her room leaving behind a lingering fruity soap smell in the air. I stared at the back of her bare calves, and went in to take my own shower. Had a good run at myself in there. Cold water did nothing to abate the horniness that's becoming increasingly more insistent every time we have these brief exchanges.

It's the first time a woman has wanted to get away from me. She always leaves first. It's intriguing and irritating at the same time.

I shrug to Justin and add, "All good so far."

"You gonna hit it?" he asks.

Jason is staring at me like he wants to know, too.

"Nah." I take another sip because the truth is I don't know. Plus it's none of Justin's business. I don't want to explain why I haven't already. It's been almost three weeks she's been living in my home. It's weird having a woman there, but even weirder that I'm starting to like it. "Want rent paid on time."

They both grin, and Jason calls me out. "You don't need the money, Jake. Who do you think you're kidding here?"

"We know you. What's up with the girl?"

I shrug again and pop the last fry in my mouth. "Not interested."

"She's not hot then?"

"Nah."

As he mutters a disappointed, "Huh. Oh well." Justin searches for a server so he can order a meal. My saying she wasn't hot is enough to switch him over to his favorite subject—politics—and he launches right into what he's going to change.

I'm normally interested, but now my mind is on her.

"I'm goin' to bed, Jake. 'Night."

"You don't wanna watch a movie?"

"Umm," she smiled, shaking her head a little as a bare foot rested on the other, toes bent and awkward. *"No. I have to interview for jobs again tomorrow. I want to be rested. Thanks, though."*

"Raincheck then."

She whispered, "Sure," but didn't mean it.

When I rented to her it was out of pity only, because I knew for a fucking fact that I wanted to fuck her, and that wasn't going to work out well since I have no intention of being monogamous AND it's kinda hard to hide being with other women when one's living in your home.

But then she went and cried. That crushed, stumbling speech of hers melted my insides.

She looked like her puppy got killed and I couldn't turn her away at that point.

The second she left I thought, *Oh shit, Jake. You fucked up. She's going to be a clingy, needy, hurt little bird and you've just set a precedent for being a softy when she cries. She's going to be sobbing every damn time she wants something.*

Never ever expected her to be mostly absent, always in her room when she's home, always out looking for work when she's not. She hasn't asked me for a thing, and her eyes haven't been red in over two weeks.

"Where you from, Drew?"

"Small town. Didn't I tell you Dublin? Yeah, small place. Quaint, but...Goodnight!"

"Hey Drew, what are you doing today?"

"Oh, don't worry about me. You have a good day at work, okay?"

"Your phone is buzzing, Drew."

"I've got it! Thank you."

Then she zips off every time like she forgot to feed

the secret hostages she's hiding in her room or something.

It's making me want to steal her phone and read what's on it. And that ain't like me at all. But...she's interesting.

Only one night did I succeed in getting her to hang out with me, and watch some T.V. But I had to trick her.

I didn't ask her a single question about herself.

I didn't ask her to watch my favorite show—I just put it on.

I didn't ask if she wanted my legendary ribs—I just put out two plates.

And I remembered she loves garlic, so I made sure the veggies had some.

It was like earning the trust of a wild, abused animal. I loved every second of it.

"Jake!"

Swaying from the stinging punch my arm receives out of nowhere, I come back to the present with a surprised, "What?!"

The twins are staring at me.

Justin barks, "I've been talking to you for fifteen minutes!"

Glancing to the table, I see their beers are empty. "Sorry. We've got this problem at the site. Waiting for a permit and the city isn't budging." I hand him my beer. "Want the rest of this? I'm gonna head home."

Jason grabs it first.

Justin throws him a look. "You're fucking quick."

"Years of practice," he grins.

Justin turns back to me. "When I get in there, things will be different."

"Fix the fucking potholes." Jason grumbles.

"Amen to that," I nod, rising up and pulling out my wallet. I love Atlanta but the potholes are nuts. "And thank God you took the bar exam before Vortex sues you for what you just did in their closet."

"And risk the cooks walking in? It was the ladies bathroom. Left stall. Handicapped. Nice and big." He grins at me. "We gave the women who came in something to dream about later."

"Dick."

Jason motions for me to put my cash away. "I've got the tab, Jake."

Justin leans forward. "Yeah, let him get this one, since times are so tough you can't fuck your roommate for fear of losing rent money."

Chuckling, I shoot back, "Go lick another waitress's pierced clit so your mouth can have a purpose."

Their laughter fades as the distance grows between us.

My smile does, too.

I've got one thing on my mind now, and one thing only: *I wonder if Drew is home.*

5

DREW

"*T*omorrow, Daddy."

"Where is it?"

"Construction company, I think. They work with water plants, desalination and things like that. They're looking for administrative help."

"Well, that's a good place to work. We need to find better ways to turn salt water into drinking water, yes we do...but Drew, you've never had a job!"

Tucked into Jake's overstuffed grey couch—my favorite place in the whole world—I stare out the window into darkness. It's been so hard finding a job with an empty resume. Much harder than I had anticipated. There is always someone more qualified than I am. I've submitted online. I've walked them in. I've even returned to some places I applied, to make sure they didn't fire the person they hired instead of me. I would take their place with only gratitude and no ego. If only someone would give me a chance.

When I got the call from Likuss, that they wanted to see me tomorrow, I almost screamed.

"Daddy, I worked at that sandwich shop in high school."

"How does that apply?"

"I'm just sayin' I had a job."

"Drew..." He trails off and we sit in silence for the most painful of minutes.

The problem is he's voicing everything I'm already thinking. I'm terrified to get my hopes up, knowing they're *not* going to hire me at Likuss, just like they've turned me away everywhere else! I don't have a chance in hell of winning that job over other applicants.

I don't need my father making me feel worse, that I know for sure. He doesn't have to tell me I have no experience.

What's going to happen to me?

Is there anything good in my life?

A key turning in our front door makes me fly off the couch. "I have to go, Daddy!"

I have been successful at one thing: avoiding the sexy beast I live with. It's been crazy difficult to remain this distant, but it's the best way for me to keep this apartment and not throw myself into his gorgeous, muscular arms—especially with my needing comfort.

And those hands!

Who wouldn't want them disappearing under her dress?

Much as I hate to admit it, the baby-maker below

my belly keeps whispering that Jake Cocker's eyes would look fabulous on my future son.

My father calmly says, "Tell Bernie I said hello."

"I will. Bye!" I hang up, running toward my room.

The front door swings open.

I have no choice but to freeze and strike a casual pose or look like a crazy person. I manage to do both.

Jake walks in wearing blue jeans and a white t-shirt that hugs his pecs. He's pulling off his brown jacket as long, dark eyelashes narrow with suspicion. "Why were you running?"

"I wasn't runnin' anywhere."

"You're panting."

Over-chuckling, I make a ridiculous face. "I am most certainly NOT."

"I could *make* you pant."

We stare at each other. My fake-smile disappears. His expression is totally serious...for all of two seconds.

A gorgeous grin spreads on his face. "Kidding, Drew."

"Oh. Ha." Fiddling absently with my phone, I picture our child running up and calling him, *Daddy!*

Now is not the time to stand here.

The truth is, it's been *hard* to think of him as too young for me with his voice as low as it is, him built like that, those muscles, and the fact that he doesn't act young. I was expecting him to be up late smoking pot and playing video games, but Jake watches movies I like, shows I need to catch up on, and he's always in bed on the weeknights by ten o'clock. He's off to work by seven, Monday thru Friday, and he keeps the house clean. I have yet to see this maid he claimed to have. I think he secretly cleans the bathroom himself. I've watched him wash his pots and dishes after every meal he's cooked for himself. And that's the other thing, he cooks real meals!

"Oh, that smells good."

"I like to make ribs on Sundays," he proudly told me.

"Like, it's a tradition?"

As he slathered on BBQ sauce, he replied with a distracted, "Mmhmm."

I sat down on the barstool by his kitchen island— still doesn't feel like mine—and watched him cut cauliflower, brussel sprouts and white onions, and throw them into a bowl for sautéing when the ribs were ready. Then he licked a thick fingertip and muttered to himself, "Almost forgot the garlic." He peeled and minced an actual garlic clove, all the while wearing no shirt and jeans that begged to be ripped off. His ass in those jeans—a poem to the male form.

And the best part about it was that, because he was busy focusing, he didn't ask me the questions he's taken to asking more and more. I was able to just sit with him and not let him get too close. That was the one and only night where I sat on the couch with him. We watched two back-to-back episodes of his favorite guy-show.

And I didn't try to escape.

Big mistake.

I realized later that the lazy, Sunday evening made

me want to spend more time with him. It's been torture to live here, but if you asked me to move out, you'd have to drag me, kicking, screaming and biting your hands. Guess that makes me a masochist.

Perhaps life isn't as bad as I've been feeling it is, since I have him so nearby.

Don't think that, Drew!

Don't get attached.

He's not a friend.

He'd not your lover.

He's a safe place to lay your head.

That's all.

I mean, not him...the apartment you share with him is safe. But laying your head on his lap wouldn't be so bad, would it? Just curling up in his arms with the television humming in the background as you breathed him in?

Clearing my throat, I mutter, "I'm going to bed. Goodnight, Jake."

"It's eight-thirty."

"I have a job interview in the morning."

His face lights up with genuine interest, and I'm so lonely for company.

"You do? Well, that's great. What's it for?"

Painfully, I whisper, "I don't want to talk about it, if that's alright."

Disappointment — or was it annoyance? — flickers across his face. He shoves his hands into his front pockets. He seems to do that every time he's unhappy. "Well, keep me company a little while, Drew. I was just with the twins and I could use some female energy for a change."

"Like you lack in female company," I dryly mutter.

"Have you seen any women here?"

Truth is, I haven't. I'm not looking forward to the day when I do, I know that.

I smile, "Just when I look in the mirror."

He grins, "Exactly. Come here."

Reluctantly, I follow him, my eyes drifting to his cute butt. Biting my lip, I force my gaze back up as he produces a bag of microwaveable popcorn from a cupboard.

"You have brothers?" I ask, leaning against the granite counter. The way he said 'twins' made me realize I'd assumed he just had the one.

"Yep. Five." He throws the bag in and sets the cook-time.

"Six boys? Are your parents Catholic?"

Jake laughs as he grabs two beers from the fridge. "I think they were hoping for a girl. They didn't get one."

"I would say not!" I'm watching his muscles flex as he pops the tops and hands me one. "Six boys. Wow. Where are you in that?"

"Second to last." He counts on his fingers. "Jaxson, Jerald, but we call him Jett now. Then there's Jason and Justin, they're identical twins. Me then Jeremy."

"All Js."

Jake taps his bottle to mine and smirks like he's mentally stripping me naked. "You have siblings, right?"

"Only child."

How I wish I had a different answer to that question. I've always wanted a bigger family. There were a lot of lonely days growing up an only child, especially with my father pulled away at all hours of the night to talk to troubled people. A pastor's work literally is never done. Dinner was interrupted frequently. Then it would be just me and Momma, because his talks would invariably go on into the late hours every time. It's probably why I married so young—I hoped it meant I wouldn't be alone wondering how 'love' could equal 'absent.'

I was in denial when Edward started not coming home at night. I'd married my father, only Edward's attention wasn't divided by his service to the Lord. It was in service to a woman I'd seen many times at the grocery store, the mall, our church. It wasn't until I caught her looking at me one too many times that I began to realize I was a fool.

Jake brings me back to the present by asking, "They didn't want more kids?"

Playing with my bottle, I sigh, "They tried. Guess God didn't want it for us." I glance down and take a sip, reading the label for the first time: Orpheus. "Is this local?"

"The only beer I drink is made here in Georgia."

I love the pride shining off him. "That's very loyal of you, Jake."

He nods. "Runs in my blood."

We stare at each other in a silence so charged I hear chemistry humming.

I will not sleep with Jake Cocker.

I need this fresh start too badly.

Also, I am not the sleep-around kind.

I never have been.

But then he reaches over and tucks a long lock of hair behind my ear and steps closer to me, his calloused fingertips lingering on my neck. I hold my breath as my ovaries scream to let him do what he wants. The goosebumps he inspired are whispering the very same thing.

His eyes darken with an intended kiss as my throat goes dry with warring desire and fear.

"Don't do this, Jake."

"Do what?" he murmurs, staring first at my lips, then into my eyes.

He's stunning close up.

Oh, why aren't my feet walking away?!

Maybe it's because I'm throbbing in my panties.

Has that ever happened before? Turned on just by proximity, a heated stare, parted lips I can feel the warmth from? His fingers brush my neck once more.

"You're lookin' at me like I'm a..."

He leans so close I can smell beer's sweetness on his beautiful lips. "Like you're what, Drew? A soft cat I want to pet?"

"Are you implying something with that?" I whisper.

"Am I meaning your *pussy* when I say cat? Yes, I mean your, hot, sopping wet, tight little pussy." I gasp, eyes widening. He pauses and adds, "But I want to do more than just pet it."

"Oh my God," I moan, and my lips stay open, ready for the inevitable.

My chance to run is gone.

I am his slave now because I made the mistake of staying when I should have disappeared. This is what I've avoided so carefully. This is my fault, yet I cannot move. My body won't let me even when my mind is screaming to run.

Jake is so sexy, so off-limits, and smells so damned good, that I am drenched with need for him to fill me with that enormous cock I can't forget he's got.

Every night that I see him walking shirtless to the couch with his home-cooked dinner, I think about that monster between his legs. Then I successfully make a break for it.

There's no running now.

I want him. I *need* him.

He will be the first man since my husband. And Edward was the first ever.

I secretly—no, *desperately*—want someone other than my cheating husband to be my only lover. Jake is perfect for the job. He's too young for me. He's a player from everything he said about having girls over as often as he pleased. I can remain detached, play it casual. A lot of people do that, don't they? Sure I've never been one of them...but I can change!

Maybe I won't fall in love with him.

Don't be stupid, Drew. Walk away. You will fall for

him. You're already hyper-sensitive to every move he makes. You really think it will get any easier if you feel his strength pressing between your thighs? If you let him touch you where you wish he would, you really think his hot kisses won't haunt you every second of every waking hour? You think you won't have to move out when it all blows up in your face?

Oh God.

I don't care.

I need him.

"Drew, I can tell you want me, too. The way you're looking at me is saying everything."

I whisper, "No, I really don't," right before he brushes his lips against mine and I moan.

Turned on by the sound, he growls, "Fuck. You know what I'm gonna do to you? I am gonna lick that cunt until you can't walk. I'm going to suck on your clit until you don't want to run away from me anymore. I will slide my tongue in and out of your tight little pussy until you beg me to fuck you and give you a release. Imagine how good my hot breath will feel down there, Drew. Just let your mind wander around that image a second for me." He turns my face to whisper with his deepest voice into my ear, "I will make you scream."

The microwave beeps.

Jake steps back and looks over at it.

I take the opportunity to escape, quietly placing the beer down and sliding my backside against the granite island until I'm safely away. I can feel him watching me but I do not look back for fear of losing my resolve.

"I have to get up early, Jake. I'm sorry, but I need this job."

Before I shut my door, with my body pulsing its anger, desire, and disgust, I glance toward the kitchen. I guess I was expecting to see him standing there at the end of the hall by my bathroom, glaring at me for leaving him like that, but instead I hear him still in the kitchen, swearing at himself, "Fucking idiot, Jake. You just had to push it."

I shut my door as quietly as I can.

6

JAKE

The popcorn gets thrown in the trash without being opened. I grab onto the countertop and grip it, growling to myself. Am I pissed that I tried to kiss her or that she rejected me? Fucking both.

She was going to let me. I know she was.

At least, I think so.

Fuck!

Downing a few glugs of my beer, I slam it on the counter and head for my room. "Night, Drew!" I call toward that always-closed bedroom door.

Her muffled, sweet voice calls back, "Night!"

Dammit, I want to knock on that wood.

Planting my hands on the nearest wall, I brace myself against the desire crackling through my torso. I wasn't expecting this. I hadn't planned on the seduction attempt and I sure as shit didn't plan on its failure.

I'm all riled up and rock-hard.

I want to touch her again.

Her hair smelled like heaven.

Her eyes, they kill me.

She's so vulnerable to everything I say, it's like we're dancing every time we speak to each other. I step forward and she steps back. I go back, and she...

Fuck!

Not knowing what to do with all this heat, I start pacing around the living room. Our living room. It used to be mine, and now a woman lives with me! How did this happen?

Let it go, Jake.

You don't want her this bad.

Your cock is lying to you.

He hasn't touched anyone in too long.

It's not that Drew's special.

Don't even go there.

She's a mystery you want to solve—that's it. Once you fuck her, you'll have figured out the puzzle she is, know what that sweet, elusive pussy tastes like, how hot her kisses are when she allows you in, and that'll be that.

I've driven myself into this frenzy and now I want to go knock on her damn door and try harder.

Harder.

The longer we talked the harder I got.

It started off innocent on my part. Never meant for this to happen. I thought maybe we'd watch a movie, have some popcorn, and I could find out about her mysterious life. But then I walked in and saw her running to her room with her braless tits bouncing, and how pretty she looked when I told her about my brothers. My cock woke up and took over.

She was relaxed, and I had to go and blow it.

But I know for a fact that if she'd have let me kiss her, it would have been worth the try.

FUCK!

I walk to her bedroom and knock. After seconds that feel like months, she calls out, "Yes?"

Let me in.

Come sleep in my room.

Hell, let's just fuck on the couch, or against this wall, or anywhere you want. Just let me into your body. Take your wall down and let me in. I've got things to show you.

Through gritted teeth, I say, "Good luck on the job interview."

"Thank you, Jake. Sweet dreams."

"You too."

Even though there's nothing else to say, I'm waiting for a reply from her. Who am I kidding? I'm really just standing here hoping for footsteps and a turning doorknob, followed by a night in her arms.

I head for my room and accidentally slam the door.

Didn't mean to do that.

Cringing, I pace around my room, hoping she didn't hear the slam and knowing she probably did.

This hard-on won't go down! My stomach is clenched and my balls are tight. Unzipping my pants, I free myself with a long grunt of relief. These jeans were too tight for all this. I grab a wall with my free hand, leaning forward and closing my eyes as I stroke my length as rough as I want to.

Knock knock. "*Can I come in?*"

"*Fuck yeah, you can. Get your sweet Georgia ass in here and get on your knees.*"

She goes down without objection, staring up at me like she does, like I'm a god and she worships me.

"*Open your mouth, baby.*"

She licks and moistens her lips up for me, then looks at my cock with need as her tits heave, the nipples hard as always.

"*You want this?*"

"*I want to suck it until you cum in my mouth,*" *she whispers, eyes always on my cock.*

"*Dirty fuckin' mouth.*"

"*Very dirty. Can you cum in my mouth, Jake?*"

"*You know I can,*" *I groan.*

She closes her eyes and opens her lips, waiting for me to fuck that mouth and then move to her pussy where I'll finish the job.

Her tongue is a slippery slice of heaven. She wraps her lips around my cock, grabs my ass with both hands and no shame, and takes me in as far as she can. She's licking and sucking my length so good that firecrackers go off in my balls.

I can feel her moaning, so happy to give me pleasure knowing I'll do the same to her and more.

I start fucking her mouth slowly then faster. She works with me, loving it. She cups my sack and gently holds it as she licks. I yell out at the fire shooting into my groin, a thick burn that will engulf both of us until she lies in my arms, boneless, spent. She teases me with a fingertip just under my sack, in that tender place. Unable to believe how good this feels, I grab her head and hold her still while I move inside her mouth, working my cock into a red-hot frenzy. I cry out as my hot cum spills into her.

"There's that bath, baby. Swim in it," I growl.

She looks fucking beautiful.

The room comes into focus and I shake my head, looking around for a towel.

"Why'd I invite this fucking hell into my life?" I mutter, wiping myself off and leaping onto the bed. As it bounces, I pick up the remote.

I can't keep living this way.

I'm going to have to do something.

This just isn't working out.

7

JAKE

*S*oft singing emanates from the bathroom as I trudge into our kitchen, hung the fuck over from lust-frustration. I glance over to the pretty sound of her voice, and pause.

She's getting ready for her interview already? It's only six o'clock in the fucking morning.

A couple words get skipped in her song and she hums through parts she doesn't know.

Give me a break.

I need coffee and I need it *now*.

I can't take the sweetness of that woman this early in the morning when I woke up rock-hard.

Again.

Well, well, well. Surprise, surprise.

Coffee's already brewed?

It's my lucky day.

The bathroom door opens, followed by the light padding of damp, bare feet as she heads toward me.

Turning around, I lean against the countertop and offer a small nod to my tormentor. "Mornin' roomie."

She pauses, hair wet and smelling of tantalizing girl-shampoo. A pink robe is held loosely closed by a slender belt that she pulls tighter the instant her blue eyes land on me.

"You don't have to do that," I smirk.

A blush rises as she blinks toward the coffee, her goal. "I didn't know you were awake."

"I'm always awake by this time. You know that."

She nods. "I didn't know it was already six. I woke up at four."

"If you go to bed at eight-thirty that's what's gonna happen."

Another distracted nod as she runs pretty fingers down her long, wet hair, smoothing it. "About last night, Jake..."

"Here it comes."

Faltering slightly, she walks to the coffee and looks at me like she's expecting me to move.

I ain't budgin.'

She pulls down two cups and has to reach over me to get at them. Somehow she makes this awkwardly graceful. Her face has all the awkward.

I watch her pour for both of us while I indulge and torture myself by staring at her ass. The robe is silky and makes it look highly spankable. Rub-able. Kiss-able. I want to mount the fucking thing.

Like now.

I groan. Don't mean to, but I do. Because her hair

smells so good and her body is so damn beautiful. She blushes at the drop of a dime. *And* she's making me coffee?

Yet I can't touch her.

This sucks.

Drew looks over, cocks an eyebrow at me.

"Can I talk to you?"

I shrug, "Yeah."

"I shouldn't have run out of here like that."

Now it's my turn to raise an eyebrow. "Oh?"

"I should've told you how I was feelin' instead. No, don't roll your eyes. I don't mean burstin' into tears and getting all girly on you again. Calm down." An amused smile tugs at her naked, pink lips. "I just mean that I *am* attracted to you, Jake. I am. You should know that."

I set the cup down, and rest my hands on the counter, elbows bent. Am I bracing myself? How much of a hold does this woman have on me? I lick my lips and hold her gaze until she's good and fidgety. "Go on, Drew."

She flushes deeper pink. With the amount of blushing she does, I have to wonder, *was she in a cave all these years?*

"The truth is any woman would be attracted to you. Despite your cocky attitude and huge ego."

I can't help but chuckle. "Uh...thanks?"

"But those things don't matter to me now. I'm not interested in pure animal attraction. I am trying to do something here and I won't let a man derail me again." She glances away and frowns.

75

Now she's got me curious. Who's the guy who unhinged her before? The one getting in my way? The idea of another guy having more of an effect on her than I've had makes me itch.

She motions to my bare chest. "You could be walking around naked and I *still* would make myself resist you, because I am in Atlanta to create a life for myself and I need to keep my head on straight. I wouldn't be able to do that if you and I were to... become sexually involved. I'm not the casual-sex type, Jake. I'm just not. I'm very grateful for the room and the peaceful nights, so please don't take it personally that I'm rejecting your advances." At my gritted teeth, she quickly adds, "Oh, don't make that face! I feel bad."

Again I laugh, but this time with heavy sarcasm. "Good talk."

Picking up the coffee, I head out.

I'm pissed now, and I *almost* leave without a word.

But my ego won't let me.

Turning slowly around, I level on her. "Drew, let me save you from feeling sorry for me. It would have been a mercy fuck had I taken you to my bed. Good luck on your interview."

Her jaw drops and I walk out.

As soon as I'm in my room, I set the coffee down, rake my fingers through my hair and swear under my breath, "Fucking shit motherfucker dammit all to hell."

8

DREW

*F*uck him! As if his bed were some kind of gift!

I was tempted last night—I even dreamt about him —but not anymore!

I stomp to my bedroom, throwing a look toward his along the way. His door is closed.

How the hell am I going to live under these circumstances?

I was simply trying to have a conversation like two adults.

"Jake, that was rude and uncalled for!" I shout with a lot more volume than I knew myself capable of.

Muffled, he shouts back, "Truth is the best policy!"

I scream, "Screw you!" running into my room.

His door opens and he shouts, "Not if you begged me!"

"Oh my God!"

That bastard is using my own words against me!

I run out of the bedroom to give him a piece of my mind and scream when I discover him standing buck naked in his doorway, smirking and crossing his arms as I come into view.

"Problem, Drew?"

"Just a little one," I hiss.

He tenses and looks down. There is nothing little about his cock, but I got him to look.

"It's not hard!"

"I meant your brain! I could care less about your enormous cock!"

His face is a battle of anger and confusion. "Fuck you!"

A triumphant grin spreads from my stomach on up. "Not if you begged me. Ha! Those are my words! MINE!"

I spin around and run to my room, slamming the door as hard as I can.

His slam in the distance echoes mine. I pace around my room wondering what to do with myself now! I left my coffee in the kitchen, and boy do I need it.

I haven't eaten.

My makeup isn't applied.

My hair is wet.

I have a job interview in...three hours.

Is that enough time to get my head on straight?

"See, this is the problem with men!" I grumble under my breath. "They are huge distractions!"

It's very clear that as soon as this month is up, I have to move out.

I sit on my bed, head in my hands until the slam of the front door lets me know the jerk has finally left for work.

I hate that man.

I really, really hate him.

9

JAKE

"We're gonna be sending you to Colorado," Don informs me as I walk into his office.

I freeze, hard hat swaying in my fingers. "Denver?"

"Yeah." He returns to shuffling diagrams of the desalination plant we're replacing sand in, looking for something he lost, distracted as he explains, "Dwight's gone back to boozing."

"Shit, Uncle Don," I mutter, dusting off my khakis as I watch him finally discover the paper he needs.

"Aha!" Looking up, triumph falters at my expression. "Jake, I know you don't want to leave your family, but we need someone there I can rely on. That's you."

"That's a hell of a compliment." Looking at my hat, I rub a spot off it and add, "You can count on me."

"I know that. You know how to run my company almost as well as I do."

"I don't know about that. Jobs maybe, but not the whole umbrella."

He leans back in his desk chair. "Don't be so modest. Working for me since you were fifteen has taught you more than you realize. I want Dwight to get his act together. He's goin' through a rough patch after what happened."

"Damn tragedy."

"Yeah. Worst kind of thing that can happen to a man," Uncle Don agrees. "And I think he just needs some time, so I'm not willing to hire someone new to take his position. You'll go there and run things until he gets sober again."

That could take years. Who knows when a guy will kick a habit?

"Right," I mutter. "Well, that's real good of you."

"You know I like to give people a chance, Jake. The only thing that's important is our relationship to other human beings. It's what's matters. He needs a helping hand. We're going to give it to him."

I nod and head to my office, feeling like I've been punched and can't fight back.

My family roots are strong.

I've never lived outside of Atlanta.

I'm not like Jett who lives a ramblers life. He would die if he couldn't ride around the states fighting battles for the innocent, and doesn't mind that it means having a home in Louisiana with his motorcycle club in order to do that. Plus he doesn't get along with Dad, but I do.

Hell, I bet Jett loves living as far away from our father as he can.

But not me. Keep me in Atlanta until I'm dust and call me a happy man. I can't believe I'm leaving.

Jeremy just left the country.

It'll be three brothers gone with me in Denver.

I heard it's pretty, but what the hell am I gonna do in Colorado? I don't know anybody there. I won't even be in the same state as my family now. They're going to like this even less than I do.

And Drew.

What about her?

She just moved in. What am I going to do about her? Keep my apartment, let her live there on her own while I continue to pay half the rent? Where would she go if I had to give the place up because I never came back?

Where am I putting my truck? Do I drive it all the way to...of course I will. That's the first answer—the only answer—I've got as soon as the question is asked.

Many more hover in my mind as Uncle Don shouts after me, "You're interviewing an administrative assistant in half-an-hour!"

❧

I'm reviewing notes on the Denver job-site, trying to prepare for what my future holds, when I hear three voices in the main office—Uncle Don, Juan, and a quiet female.

Time flew. I straighten up while cutting a quick glance to the wall-clock on my left, thinking I'm not ready for this, and yet the click of heels grows louder.

A hasty sip of coffee readies my mind for meeting the new candidate. Uncle Don likes me to conduct the initial interviews because he's a big softie and, if he had his way, he'd hire everyone who came through the door. We give a lot of chances to people with little experience or bad pasts, because of his desire to help. It's an admirable trait that has gotten him into trouble —so he finally admitted I should screen applicants first. I'll still give good ones their shot. But I can spot and block a disaster, too. Saves the company money training someone who won't carry their weight, and who weighs down and angers the rest of our hard-working crew.

As I set down the cup of Joe, fingers moving to rest on my old calculator out of habit, I feel lukewarm caffeine sliding down my throat, and a tightness to my jaw. Can't deny I dislike the fact that whoever gets hired for this position will stay in Atlanta while I'll move to a state where I know no one, away from a family I love more than myself, and who I see nearly every damn day.

I'm not looking forward to this.

Any of it.

The interview.

The move.

None of it.

Heels stop in my doorframe, and my blood freezes.

Drew's jaw drops as she blinks at me with stunned silence.

A devilish smile spreads as my heart-rate speeds up. "Good morning. I'm Jake Cocker." I stand, reach over my organized desk, extending the same calloused fingers that caressed her neck just last night.

She accepts my offered hand and shakes it like she wishes she could use it to punch me. "Nice to meet you, Mr. Cocker. I'm Drew Charles."

"That's a boy's name."

"So I've heard."

I'm still gripping her hand. She tugs to retrieve it, but I pull her a little closer to whisper, "This is going to be fun."

I let go.

War is swirling, the same war I left her with when I stormed out this morning. My quick-to-blush roomie is bright red, struggling with whether or not she should leave me, and the job, behind.

We stare at each other.

My smirk grows.

Her nostrils flare as angry blue eyes flick toward my office door. She decides to sit down, which earns both my respect and amused anticipation.

I take my seat and lean back with an even bigger smile.

Uncle Don appears in my office, oblivious as he drops her resume on my desk. I glance to the almost blank sheet of paper that bears her name at the top.

Uncle Don gives her a big smile, only his isn't tainted with I'm-going-to-fuck-with-you.

"You're in good hands with my nephew, Mrs. Charles."

Mrs. Charles? I glance to Drew. Her eyes are ice blue now even as she tries to smile at him. It's the most tense show of teeth I've ever seen, and I almost laugh. But my brothers and I are champions at fucking with people, so I contain the laughter, bide my time for the fun to begin as soon as he's gone.

He turns to me, crossing his arms, yellow button-up shirt crinkling at the elbows. "Jake, Drew here doesn't have much in terms of experience, but her email was charming, so I wanted to bring her in to see what you thought of her." He smiles between us. "Well, I'll leave you to it. Heading to the job site for an hour or so." He looks at Drew. "Mrs. Charles, I probably won't see you after your interview, but I know Jake will tell me how it went. Good luck."

"Thank you," she smiles.

"Oh, don't be nervous! Jake's a good guy."

"I'm sure he is. I'm not nervous."

Uncle Don glances to me with a look that says he's no dummy. He's aware she's lying, but there's always anxiety at job interviews, so he winks at me to go easy on her, and walking out, bellows in his gregarious-good-guy way, "Juan! Let's go, buddy. I don't have all day!"

Drew and I are locked onto each other as oxygen crackles around us. Her chest expands on a long inhale. My skin is itching, but I'm not showing it.

Mrs.

What the fuck?!

"Let's just wait for them to leave. Then I'll begin."

"Fine," she smiles, teeth gritted. "Let me have it."

Boots clomp around the main room as Uncle Don forgets his keys in his office, then grumbles that he had them in his pocket the whole time. Drew blinks quickly toward the door, straightens up even more, and locks onto me again. She's so damn pretty when she's pissed. My mind is on the name he called her, because what the fuck? He didn't make a mistake with that *Mrs.* and I have to find out more.

We hear the sound of the front door closing.

Silence.

Nobody left here but us.

10

DREW

*W*hat a relief after the hell I went through with Jake that morning to meet Don Likuss — a sweet, bear of man with an open smile. He insisted I use his first name when I addressed him, which put me at ease as he informed me that his nephew would be conducting my interview.

On the drive here, I spent every ounce of energy avoiding thoughts of Jake by mentally reviewing notes I'd taken on how to answer interview questions in a manner that showed I was at once capable, interested, amiable, and reliable...even without experience.

Smile when you're nervous.

Smiles put people at ease.

Even you.

Ask the interviewer questions about themselves, like you're talking to an older relative whom you hold in high regard. It shows interest and curiosity, two very important traits. You're also learning about them, if you'd like to work for them. Interviews go both ways.

But I knew when I highlighted that passage that all I needed was a job. Even if I hated my future boss, I'd stick with it in order to change my life. Then I'd upgrade employment after I'd proven myself worthy of more, and had something valuable on my resume: *experience.*

As I walked through a simple office with black and white photographs of complicated construction sites framed and hung on scuffed beige walls, I flicked through as many memorized passages as I could stuff in my mental toolbox, hoping that when the need arose, I'd recall them in an instant.

Never speak with the familiarity of a friend at this stage—it shows a lack of respect to the employer's position. Even if they get very casual, remain smiling and professional, hold back to let them know you're conscious of their status. You might talk yourself out of a job if you come off as undisciplined or annoyingly chatty.

An employer wants to know if you'll cost or make them money. That's the only reason to give you a job—if you add value to their business and help it, your boss, and your co-workers, continue to thrive. It doesn't matter if you're pushing paper, a broom, or a million dollar idea through a pipeline, being someone who does good work and is easy to be around, will keep you securely on the payroll for a long time.

I'd read a book aimed at college students entering

the job market, to prepare myself because even at my age *that* is what I am—a newcomer.

Nothing was going to stop me from getting a job. Hopefully this one.

Make yourself indispensable, the book said.

What's more valuable than hard work, a great attitude, and a willingness to do everything it takes?

I stepped into the office doorway and almost had a heart attack. There behind a spotless desk was my bastard roomie with his thick fingertips resting absently on an old-fashioned calculator.

So much for preparation!

I almost flipped right around and left.

All that vowing about wanting the job even if I hated my boss flew out of the window. The idea of working for this obstinate, rude beast was abhorrent! His devil-is-coming-to-get-you smirk warned me that oh was I in for the interview of my life. He'd toy with me and toss me into the parking lot after he'd had his fun. And then I'd have to see him at our home tonight. No thank you!

But I learned something about myself during those strained seconds in which we shook hands and it is this: I have some fight in these bones. Drew Charles is no coward!

Bring it on, Jake.

Bring.

It.

On.

As we wait for Don Likuss to remember his keys

are in his pocket, I lock onto the stormy brown eyes of my roommate. The sound of the door clicking shut brings unnerving silence swarming around us like angry bees you can feel but can't hear.

With a sweet southern smile I cross my legs, steel my jumping nerves, and start the game. "Well, Mr. Cocker, I didn't expect such a nice surprise."

"I agree, *Mrs.* Charles. So...let's see." He lifts my pathetic resume and reads the sheet as slowly as if it were written in Portuguese. "How long have you been married?"

So that's how he's going to play it.

"I'm not sure that my marital status matters when it comes to job performance."

"Loyalty plays into everything."

Bristling, I hiss, "I am extremely loyal, Jake..." and pause, not willing to lose the war yet. Hastily gathering all the self-control I can muster, I correct myself through a gritted smile, "...*Mr. Cocker.*"

His eyebrows rise slightly. "It looks like you haven't worked a job other than house duties."

Inwardly I cringe but manage to hide it. In order to compose some semblance of a resume, I had to list what I did for Edward, because it was all I'd ever done. And frankly, though most won't give us credit for this, housewives work very hard. If anyone tells me differently, I'll set them straight, and quick.

Still smiling, I shoot back, "Running household finances *is* administrative work. Also accounting. And long and short term financial planning."

Jake doesn't say anything at first. He just stares at me with those incredibly seductive brown eyes and, for a moment, I think I've won round-one.

But he leans back in his chair, his cocky smirk making an encore appearance. "Which is why I asked how long you were married. I'd like to know the length of this rather *inventive* job experience."

My lips purse, and I hear myself confess before I even realize I'd made the decision to, "Since I was nineteen."

"And you're how old?"

"You know how old I am."

"Right. So that's how many years?"

"Don't know how to count?" I snap, leaning forward. "And with a calculator right at your fingertips. That must be very frustrating for you."

His eyes flash from hot to ice-cold.

Oh shit, I poked a sleeping polar bear.

"Are you *still* married, Drew?"

"I am."

His eyelashes fall to my resume as a wall erects around him. I can see heavy bricks slamming on top of each other quicker by the second. "I see. Well, that would have been something you could have mentioned when you shot me down this morning."

I blink in surprise at the switch from interview to home-life. Defensively I reply, "I didn't think it was your business."

Jake sucks on his teeth, still staring at the paper. I can hear his foot tapping under his desk. He's barely holding it together! And suddenly I feel terrible as he mumbles a distant, "I guess it isn't."

We sit in the worst silence I've ever experienced in my life. I'm trying to stay strong, to give as good as I get. But I'm not as seasoned at hiding my feelings as I would like to be, and I can tell he's very angry with me. So I cave, holding my head with as much dignity as I can. "I didn't say anything because we're separated... and it's very fresh and embarrassing."

His gaze drifts up and locks with mine. Heat shoots into my tummy as I watch the wall stop erecting. Was it my admitting I'm embarrassed about the impending divorce?

"How bad do you want this job?"

My lips part in surprise. "Bad."

"How bad."

"Why do you ask?"

"I want to know *what you'd do for it.*"

My eyes widen. "Well, what's that supposed to mean? Are you going to ask me to—"

"—No, Drew. I want to know how you'd approach working in a field you know nothing about."

Wringing my hands where he can't see them, I change gears. I'd assumed he was suggesting sexual favors, for obvious reasons, but this is now a real interview, and the possibility of clocking in at an actual job speeds my heart up. Our eyes lock and I earnestly launch in with the truth.

"I'm very eager to learn. And I'm smart. I will study the business, whatever aspects are most important to know first I'll focus on, and then grow from there. I'll spend time studyin' after hours, too. I know I have a lack of experience to make up for, but the person who really wants the job, and who badly needs it, will be the hardest worker. That would be me, if you give me this chance."

He is staring at me, expression unreadable while I beg to be taken seriously. To bare myself like this after sparring is so unnerving I am not prepared for, "Why are you getting divorced?"

My throat dries up.

I blink at him and swallow hard as I search for a way out of this conversation. Some memories are too difficult to dredge up. Especially with him this suspicious and downright chilly as he awaits my answer. Why must Jake push my buttons so easily? Ever since we met I've felt an excited irritation I can't put my finger on. Despite the fact that he looks furious, if someone came in here and asked me to leave, I would try to stay! What is wrong with me when it comes to this man?

"Why?!" I cry out in frustration. "*Why* do you want to know that? How does that have anything to do with being an administrative assistant?"

"*Mrs.* Charles." He tosses my resume dismissively on the desk as if the interview is over now.

I snap a crass and out of character, "Oh shit, *really*?!" sliding shaking fingers over my lap as I try to control the volcano erupting inside my core. "Okay, if you *must* know, Edward cheated on me. And from

what I gather it had been goin' on for a very long time."
I sit back in defeat. "*There!* Let me have it, Jake. Give
me the best you've got, because Lord knows I can take
more than I thought I ever could!"

His once sharp eyes have clouded over. He's
flicking his thumb with his index finger. "Your husband
cheated on you?"

"Yes!"

"After all those years."

My chest is heaving now. "Yes."

The tips of Jake's fingers slowly rest on my paltry
resume. "I'm sorry, Drew. That's fucked up."

Stunned, I stare at him.

The evil smirk, the darkened eyes, the tension in
his shoulders, they're gone. A friend is staring back at
me. The façade of interviewing a stranger vanishes as
Jake's volume drops on a deep frown. "They're sending
me to Colorado."

My stomach sinks. "You're leaving?"

Jake glances to the window and holds on it. "Yep."

"For how long?"

He shrugs, "Don't know."

"You're not happy about it?" Staring into an
unwanted future, he slowly shakes his head. I whisper,
"Oh God, Jake, I'm sorry about that." I stare at his
strong profile while searching for a way to make him
feel better, deciding taking myself out of the equation
will do the trick. On a deep inhale I offer, "Well, if it
helps, I was thinking of moving out at the end of the
month anyway, what with everything that's been goin'

on. Us bein' roommates is clearly not workin'. So you don't have to worry about me and where I'll land."

With a dismissive wave, he glances to me, lips soft and eyes so forlorn I wish I could hug him and tell him everything is going to be okay.

He exhales, "You can stay. I'm keeping my place while I'm gone. I'll pay my half," and looks back out the window, a flash of anger mixing with the sadness I saw.

Every molecule in me is screaming to go and hold him. All I can do is offer a tortured, "I'm really sorry, Jake."

"Why didn't you work?"

There's no fight in me anymore as I explain, "Edward and I worked for a long time, but then—"

He cuts me off, picking up my resume and bluntly demanding, "When you were married, why didn't *you* work?"

"Oh. Um...if I tell you, will you hire me?"

He stares at me a beat, chuckles and admits, "Depends on the answer."

A smile tugs as I cry out, "God, you're unbelievably frustrating!" I sit back in the chair, exasperated, throwing my hands up. "Edward said that mothers don't work. They should be home for the children."

Jake tosses the resume yet again, this time disgusted. "What the fuck? You have kids? Why aren't they with you?"

"Oh please!" I snap with fire burning in my eyes, my back stiffening at the implication. "If I had children they wouldn't leave my sight! I've never had the joy of bein' pregnant, Jake. There are no children waitin' for me to come home. He kept promisin' that *next* year would be the year. But then time would pass and he'd put it off again. Always when I was about to look for work of my own, gain some independence, that's when he'd reel me back in. I found out later that he'd had a Vasectomy without my knowledge. He'd been lyin' all along, just to control me." I pause and stare at my hands. "You know how I found out? Our doctor called to confirm his appointment to *reverse* the Vasectomy, which apparently they can do. Like an idiot, I asked, '*What vasectomy?*' to a doctor who'd known me since I was just a girl. It was terrible." Covering my eyes, I hold my breath to push back tears. What I'm about to say I haven't told anyone except for my parents. Not even Bernie. "To make things so much worse, he wasn't reversin' it *for me*. No, I got that call *after* he told me he was leavin' me for Debra Morales, a woman who *worked* with him, if you can believe the irony."

I am blinking away pain as I remember the pretty brunette I discovered watching me in church. That was the day I finally awoke in denial's dark bed. I knew in my gut that something was very personal about how she stared at us, and I'd seen her around before, watching me with a peculiar sort of interest, but I always ignored it. I was too naive to believe my intuition about them was right.

Forcing a laugh, I tell Jake the finale, something so horrible that I would never have believed the rumor's validity had it not come from my own momma. "She's pregnant now, this Debra person. With his daughter, I'm told. So, yay Edward. A father after all. And she's keeping her job."

Jake remained silent during my tragic tale. Patiently he listened, lips tight. My eyes widen as he rises up and comes around the desk, his khakis brushing together as his boots clomp on hardwood flooring. Confused, lips parted, I stare up at him as he gently pulls me from my chair, wrapping me into his arms and giving me a bear hug that tears my heart to pieces.

"I'm so sorry, Drew," he whispers, squeezing me harder.

The show of human kindness is too much for my jilted heart. It has been nearly impossible to remain focused on building my new life knowing how many years I wasted on a man who was deceiving me in more ways than just the affair. Depression wanted to take hold many, many times since I discovered the truth, but I refused to waste another breath from these lungs, or another minute from the finite amount I'd been given in this lifetime on anything but creating a life where I would finally be happy.

I'd stopped loving Edward long ago, but I never would have left him. Even still, there was no affection between us anymore. We may as well have slept in separate rooms, it'd been so long since we'd touched each other.

This hug is the first touch I've had from a man since...

I slip my arms around Jake's strong neck and bury my face in his shoulder, fighting back tears with all the willpower I've got. He rocks me, a friend holding another friend after hearing they've suffered terrible injustice. His voice is thick in my ear as he says, "I'm so sorry that happened to you. I'm so sorry."

I croak, coming undone, "I didn't expect you to be nice!"

"Yeah, well...I've got a soft spot for family. He was yours. He shouldn't have hurt you like that."

Jake keeps rocking me until all my muscles are puddles.

He releases me, but I'm so desperate for the comfort, I can't look away from his handsome face. I'm waiting for him to return to his seat, or tell me that the interview is over...or something! But he's silently holding my shocked gaze, his lips a firm line.

All I want is to bury myself into his strength again.

I want his arms around me a little longer.

I step closer and touch his face. He blinks behind a hard decision, then out of the blue leans in and captures me in a kiss. We stay with our lips pressed hard together as electricity courses through our bodies. His jaw unlocks and Jake claims me with the best kiss I've ever had. Our tongues dance as he fists my hair and pulls my head back to kiss me deeper. I moan into him as his hands travel down my back, taking their time before they rest on my ass. After a few heated moments he gasps for breath and stares at me.

"There's no turning back if we keep this up. Now's

your chance to keep your promise about never fucking me."

The strength of his fingers feels so good. His erection can't be ignored from its sheer size alone. As he strains against me, my tummy is tight with need.

I don't know if it's because I'll miss hearing him walk around the apartment, or that his moving away provides a solution—no chance of getting too attached when he's not even in Georgia—or maybe I just can't deny to myself anymore how much I want him. I don't know why I chose this moment of all moments, but instead of turning Jake Cocker away again, I whisper a desperate, *"Just this once."*

"Just this once, what, Drew?" he rasps into my neck as rough kisses press against shivering skin.

"Just this once...make my pain go away."

He locks eyes with me with a hunger I've never seen before in anyone. Jake Cocker takes possession of my mouth until I'm trembling. He wipes everything but the computer off his desk in one swift motion. Papers go flying. Pencils roll into corners of the room. The old calculator hits the ground with a thud as Jake plants me on the desk, separating my legs. I lace my fingers into his hair and watch him kneel in front of me to hike up my skirt. His fingers don't hesitate as they dip underneath and find my pink panties, sliding under the elastic into my secret, swollen folds as I bite back a moan.

"Fuck, you're as slippery as an oil spill in August,"

Jake groans, making me smile at such an oddly *specific* description.

Tugging my panties down my legs and tossing them without looking, he dips his gorgeous head to lick me long and slow. I've never enjoyed this act before. Edward thought it was gross, and stopped doing it early on. Part of me is terrified that Jake will recoil. With baited breath I'm watching him and realize he loves everything second of this. His groans are so sexy, his attention thorough. I can't help but open to him from the inside out, tingling more and more with each slow lick. I try not to moan just in case someone comes back to the office. But then his gravelly voice vibrates my swollen pussy as he says, "I knew you'd taste this good." I cry out as his tongue lunges deeply inside of me. I'm amazed to find my hips rising on their own, arching to offer my pussy to him completely. I throw my head back, staring at the ceiling and wondering how is he making me feel so damn sexy?

He growls, making me whimper as he asks, "You like what my tongue is doing to your cunt don't you, baby?"

The fire his filthy talk skyrockets into my core is shocking. Shyly, I moan-whisper my reply, but of course that's not good enough.

"*Tell me* you love it, Drew. Tell me how much you love my tongue flicking your swollen clit like this."

He proceeds to tease me until I'm panting and gripping his head in a vice. "Oh God, Jake!"

He pauses and breathes hot air onto me, opening

my folds with calloused fingertips as he warns, "Tell me, or I'll stop."

No, don't stop!

"I love your tongue," I moan. "Is that good? I've never talked dirty. Tell me what you want me to do!"

He smirks and starts flicking me again with the tip of his tongue. But then he stops again, the bastard, and breathes hot air on me until I'm boneless from a delicious feeling I've never known before.

"I want you to beg me to fuck you."

"I will do no such thing!"

He starts flicking again, playing my pussy like a fiddle in the backwoods of Georgia.

"*Beg* me," he growls and slides two fingers inside my tight cave, pumping steadily. He starts licking me while he does this and I am one wet hot mess under his skill. Reading every reaction, he stops just short of the sweet release that could take me over if he'd only allow it.

I cry out, "You asshole!" panting.

"*Beg* me, Drew."

His fingers slide really slowly in and out of my trembling pussy as he watches my expressions growing desperate. Lady or no, I'm about to do whatever he asks of me because I am right on the edge and he knows it.

He's torturing me on purpose, to win.

"Beg me, baby. Beg me to take you over the edge into the sweetest orgasm of your life. I'll take you there, but only if you tell me what I want you to. Then I will fill you so full with my cum that you will never want to be with another man again without thinking of *me* while *he's* inside you."

"Oh God, *stop,* Jake," I moan, out of my mind, throbbing everywhere.

He slides in and holds his fingers as deep as they'll go as he kisses my clit, then looks at me again. "First you're going to cum all over my tongue. These fingers I've buried here in your hot, wet little cunt? You're going to soak them. Then you know what I'm gonna do to you? I'm going to fuck you right here on my desk. I'm going to stretch your walls and pump between these gorgeous thighs until I fill you like I promised. Do you want it?"

"Yes!"

"Say it." He starts moving those talented fingers oh-so-slowly, holding his thumb over my throbbing clit and brushing it just a little now that I'm so sensitive.

Trembling with desperation, needing everything he's promising, I shyly moan, "Please fuck me! Please fuck me like that, Jake. I can't take it anymore!" He grins and kisses my clit again. It's torture. Crying out, I free myself of shame and moan loudly, throwing my inhibitions away. "Fuck me harder than you think you even can, Jake. Fuck me harder than you've ever fucked any other woman!!!"

Danger lights his eyes. He works me with a precision that makes me scream his name as I cum just like he promised, clenching and trembling on his gorgeous face. I've never bucked my hips before, not ever. But here I am holding his shoulders and his head, bucking against his tongue as he growls into the pussy he's trained into his slave. When I've passed the cliff, he pushes my shaking legs a little wider and gives me one last, very long lick goodbye.

I'm gasping for breath as we lock eyes.

In a daze I watch as Jake rises, unzips his fly and shoves his pants to the ground.

"I think that might hurt me."

"Probably," he smirks, grabs my ass and pulls me to the edge of his desk. As he bends his knees to position the gorgeous shaft, all of his muscles go tense. It's stunning. I open my mouth to be claimed, and as his engorged tip enters me, Jake groans, leans forward and eats me alive. With our tongues wrapped around each other's, his beautiful cock dives in with one urgent thrust. I cry out against the pleasure-laced pain, biting his lip. It's been over a year since Edward was inside me, and that was a terrible experience. My cave has gotten smaller with abuse and neglect. There were nights when I thought I'd never feel a man again, and I never imagined one like Jake. I want him like I've never wanted anyone. I can even taste myself on his tongue and I don't care. The way my heart feels with him inside me like this is too much to bear. His length is wide, long, pulsing. He'd worked himself into a frenzy by going down on me, making me cum so hard, that he stretches my walls near their breaking point, yet I love it so much the tingling speeds up all over again.

We're both panting as Jake grabs onto my ass with

one hand, my head with the other, and pushes in deeper, looking into my eyes.

"I'm going to move slowly so you can get used to me, but I won't be able to do that for long." He thrusts in and out, holding back just like he promised. I moan into his growling lips as he confesses, "I've wanted to fuck you ever since we met." Suddenly he claims my mouth with a deep kiss as his hips start to move more urgently.

Unabashedly I return his kiss, arching my hips to receive all of him, my whole body covered in tiny, happy goosebumps.

Jake breaks from my lips, buries his head in my hair and growls into my ear as his body starts moving of its own free will. "You're so fucking tight, Drew, I'm gonna cum if you don't say something that turns me *off*. I'm serious. Think of something."

I wrack my puddled brain. To make matters worse, he throws his head back, moving faster. He's so handsome. I steal a peek of where our bodies are coming together, the soft private hair blending as the base of his length comes into view with each stroke before disappearing again.

I start to whimper, "It's all too good!"

"Fuck, I can't go slow." He locks eyes with me, grimacing in sexy pain. "I'm trying, but I'm failing."

I whisper against his lips, "I don't want you to hold back," as he kisses me again. "Do anything you want!"

He growls, "Oh God," latching his mouth with mine as three hard thrusts take us over. Breaking free, he gasps, all of his muscles tightening as he tries not to cum early. "That's not helping. I'm so close. Fucking *say something* that will slow this down."

I don't know what he wants me to say!

I'm right there, too.

Why must we stop?

But I want to please him, so I search my numb brain and stammer, "Um...um..."

He snarls into my neck, pounding me harder and harder. Stopping, he pants and begs me, "Anything! Fuck. I've never cum this quickly before. Fuck. I can't stop!"

Desperate, I whisper the thing no single man wants to hear at a time like this, "I want to be pregnant."

Jake looks at me.

His eyes go hard and his teeth clench.

A roar rips from his lungs and tears through his body.

His erection expands in both girth and length and Jake loses it, pounds me so desperately, I'm in danger of tearing straight up the middle.

My inner walls shudder as I begin to cum. The tingles race up my thighs as my pussy tightens around him. I grip his head and scream as his release overtakes him, too, and he shoots into my body. Our moans are primal, thick, in different octaves, mine high pitched and his low as it will go. Our mouths latch and lock in an aching kiss as his hips thrust. Jake pounds between my thighs until there is nothing left for him to give me.

Yet, I want more.

So much more.

I throw my arms around my roommate, undone yet more awake than I've been in my entire life. He shudders and presses gasping kisses into my tender neck. After-shocks tremble from his body into mine as we hold each other.

I never knew it could be like this.

I never knew a man could feel this perfect inside of me.

I am in deep shit.

11

JAKE

I hear him before I see him.

"How'd it go with Mrs. Charles today?" Uncle Don's smiling face appears in my doorway. I'm sitting behind the desk, everything back in its place, as he adds, "Not qualified for much but seems eager to change that. You know I like to give people a shot."

Maintaining a sober expression I shuffle a few papers that don't need it. "I like her. I think she could do well here."

My uncle's eyebrows go up slightly. "That's high praise coming from a picky bastard like you."

On a shrug, I lean back to tell him with total candor, "She's got no experience, but she's never really been given a chance. Husband was old school. Didn't want her working. She's smart. She'll learn fast." It's fucking hard as hell not to grin as I add, "And you're right...she's surprisingly eager."

"Good." He smacks my doorframe and heads back

to his office, calling over his shoulder, "We'll need someone to learn paperwork now that you'll be gone."

A sucker-punch to my gut robs me of any verbal response. I'd totally forgotten I was leaving. Drew's willing, open body and that sweet little mouth of hers begging me to take her right here where I work, knowing the guys would be back soon—hell, could have walked in at any minute—let's just say it gave my mind something better to think about than moving to Denver and leaving my family behind. Way better.

I grab the phone, dial and wait for him to answer. "Jake, my boy! What's up?"

"Hey Dad." Rubbing my forehead, I close my eyes against my unlikable future. I've got nothing against Denver except it's not Atlanta. "I'm being transferred to Colorado."

"What?! Why?" He calls to my mom, "Don's sending my son to fucking Denver!"

I can't help but smile at my father swearing. The Congressman rarely does it. But he's a smart man and he put two and two together faster than his temper could react.

"Your mother wants to know why, too!"

"There's a guy running the place now who can't keep his hands off the bottle. He's been given chances but he's not taking them. Death in his family. He's a mess. I have to go run the place until..." I pause and stare off. "He didn't say how long."

Dad goes quiet. The shared silence makes this harder for me because I know he's feeling what I am—

he doesn't want me that far away. Another son gone? That's not welcome news. Jeremy just left for Syria after finishing intense training at Parris Island, South Carolina. And Jett is in a motorcycle club called The Ciphers that travels all over the country, a fact that tears Dad up because he doesn't see them for what they really are. He just sees the down and dirty lawlessness of their actions—he won't acknowledge they're doing it for the good of innocent people who cannot fight for themselves. Our father feels Jett betrayed him by living outside the law, so he pretends Jett doesn't exist. What my older brother does with his days isn't exactly bragging material at the White House.

I like staying nearby—for my old man. I respect the hell out of him and spend as much time with him as I can, around our normal lives and his busy political schedule. Then there are the twins. Since Jeremy left, that makes Jason and Justin the only brothers I can hang out with in town. Jaxson keeps to himself, living on his ranch an hour north, but if I ever need him, he's here, and I spend weekends with him sometimes.

Don't get me started about thinking of leaving Mom. She raised us to be independent, a fact that made us depend on her maybe a little more. She's like a soft rock you can steady yourself with when life's river goes rapids, one that if you let go, you know it's still there and will always be. I'll miss Uncle Don, too. He gave me this job when I was just a teenager looking to make it on my own. How will I run the Denver site without him?

This is gonna suck.

My father finally grumbles, "Let me talk to him."

"Dad, don't. I appreciate it, but I'm a grown man. I can handle what comes to me. I just wanted to tell you."

"Jake..." He exhales long and low. "Never mind. Okay, I won't talk to Don. When are you going?"

"A couple of weeks? A week? Shit, I don't know."

"Watch your mouth."

"Sorry, Sir." I wince and close my eyes as my heart aches. "Will you tell Mom the details? And make sure she doesn't try to talk Don out of it. I don't want her doing that."

Another sigh. "Yes. I don't have to tell you how she'll feel about this. If we had an end date, it would be easier to take. Maybe I could just—"

"Dad! Don't talk to him. I mean it. I'll be angry if you do that. I take care of my business, and I'll just stay there longer."

He's silent before he finally grumbles, "Fine," then his voice picks up some levity as he adds, "I guess this means we need to have a family BBQ."

Leaning back on an oh-shit grin I tell him, "Oh man, you had to throw that at me, didn't you. Yeah, I guess I'd have to go." As if I would miss it.

We both chuckle. Even though my dad and I don't have the same coloring—I take after Mom—we have the same laugh. That's something I've hung onto as a son, that connection. Hearing it today hits me pretty hard. After we say goodbye, hang up, and I set the phone down, my smile quickly fades. I know exactly how Mom will react—she'll tell all my brothers. I can just see her face as she's listening to the news, her pretty brown eyes filling with tears.

Drew's face appears, taking Mom's place. The anguish I saw as she shared how her husband's affair ended in another woman's pregnancy. How she'd wanted to have kids. How he stole that from her with a secret surgery. I can't imagine that kind of betrayal. What kind of monster holds a woman hostage like that?

Flashes of her on my desk, clawing into my back as she let me kiss her like I've never kissed anyone, hit me. I take a deep breath and push her out of my mind.

She needs to focus on her fresh start, she said.

I agree with her.

She wants more than I can give.

I wasn't planning on falling for the woman. Maybe my leaving right now is perfect timing on that front.

But for the rest of the workday, God help me, she sneaks back into my mind over and over. I keep seeing us fucking, kissing, fighting, my face in her quivering pussy as she finally dropped her inhibitions.

I don't want anything serious. I know that. The problem is I live with her. That's about as serious as you can get.

When Uncle Don sees me heading home, he

admits with a wary smile, "I expected to hear from Michael today."

I chuckle and confess, "I told him not to call you."

"Thank you for that."

"It's not his business," I shrug, crossing my arms. "But he likes having control."

"Runs in the family," Uncle Don smirks.

"Yep. Listen, I don't think I told you that Drew is my roommate. No, don't look like that. I didn't know she applied for a job here. She's been applying everywhere since she moved here, and I had no way of knowing it was her coming in, *and* she didn't know where I worked. Just that I worked in construction."

Matching my stance, his eyes narrow, "Why didn't you tell me this earlier?"

"I was really shocked to see her, I guess. And truth be told, we'd gotten into a fight this morning."

He nods and blinks to the ground. "Is that going to be a problem?"

"Nope."

"If you're fighting at home, how's it gonna be here?"

I breathe in through my teeth with a low hissing sound because I hadn't anticipated he'd see that as a problem. My head isn't on right. Hoping I didn't ruin her chances, I tell him with a steady eye, "I think we smoothed things out today." He nods like that's good news, and I add for good measure, "And I'm leaving, so it won't matter at all. She needs the job. You were right about how she'll be eager to learn and do her best."

This time I'm not inwardly smiling or thinking about sex like I was earlier today. I really do believe it and it shows through my voice as I tell him, "Drew will want to stay on and will do whatever she has to, to make that happen."

"Good," he says, thinking about it before he turns and heads to his office.

JAKE

*T*he apartment is dark when I get back.

"You home?" I call at her bedroom door, glancing to find the lights off in the bathroom, too. "Where is she?" I mutter, dropping my keys onto the untouched kitchen counter and grabbing myself a chilled, clean water from the fridge. The kitchen sink is dry and empty as if nobody has been here since I left. Did she even come home after the interview?

It's so strange that I live with a woman I just fucked. In my office. During her job interview.

Really hard to distance myself, too, because living with her is starting to feel normal.

A smile tugs at my lips and I discover that my feet are heading to her room without my permission. A rap on the door provides confirmation that she's probably not here. "Drew?" I crack the door a little, knowing full well that I haven't been in here since I planted that lamp, her sole piece of furniture, in an empty room. Leaning on the doorframe, I take it all in. She made it really homey in here. She must have had that bed-frame delivered because she never asked me to help put it together.

I walk in and touch the goose-down comforter. She's got a small table with a single chair in the corner and a book lying on it titled *Resumes For Dummies*. Lifting it up I find four personal-development books all related to business, well known success manuals. Thumbing through them I discover she's scrawled notes, in pen, on tons of the pages, circling parts, dog-earing others.

"Shit! So this is why you spend so much time in here, huh?" I mutter as I read a quote she double-underlined.

You are a summation of the five people you spend the most time with. Choose wisely.

Can't deny that I'm impressed.

I stack the books back how I found them, and glance over to a coatrack with her hats and necklaces hanging on it. In doing so, I land on a framed photo on a small four-level bookshelf next to the rack. A frown spreads throughout my whole fucking body as I walk over to it and lean down to inspect the face of a smiling man around Drew's age with his arm around her. They're at a party from the people and lights in the background—an outdoor celebration. She's smiling at the camera. He's gazing at her like there's nowhere else better in the world to look.

I know who this has got to be. But why would she keep a photo of her husband after...?

The soft turn of her key in the front door lock makes me nearly drop the photo. I shove it back on the shelf, rapidly aligning it with the dust outline its absence left behind.

The click of heels sounds for two steps and the door closes. I know she's taking off her shoes.

How the fuck am I going to explain being in her room?!

Shit! My heart is pounding.

What the hell is wrong with me?

This is so not cool, Jake.

Running an unsteady hand through my hair I take a deep breath and walk out, ready to face my own weakness head on. This ain't gonna be fun.

Her gaze drifts over to me from where she's slipping out of her heels at the mat. Her eyes widen with surprise and she glances from me to her room. Before she can say anything I grin. "Hey, I was just looking for you."

Her frown flickers and fades away. "Did you just get home, too?"

"Yep. Two seconds before you did." *So much for honesty.* But looking at her reminds me of when I smacked her ass on the way out of my office. She was grinning from ear to ear and trusted me in that moment. I'm not ready to give that up, just because I got a little curious about her. But how am I going to ask about that photograph if I don't fess up?

"Where ya been?" I smile, shoving my hands in my pockets.

Her eyes flicker to them and her smile becomes forced. "Jake, we have to talk." She sets her purse down and wrings her hands.

I exhale and mutter, "Shit. Not this again. Just so you know, I was going to tell you we have to talk, too." She stares at me, and I admit, "Okay, that came out sounding childlike."

She smiles and makes my chest tighten because she's so fucking beautiful. I didn't think so, at first. Pretty, yeah, sure. I *knew* she was fuckable, but now the woman has grown on me in a way that's becoming harder to ignore.

Except for these fucking talks.

"Okay, go ahead," I grumble, leaning on the wall and crossing my arms.

She glances to my biceps and pauses. I flex them just to tease her. She smiles wider. "Nice. Stop that."

"Stop this?" I pump them back and forth, make them dance for her benefit. "This thing? Stop being charming? Have you seen my cock? Because that's the finale."

She stifles a laugh. "Okay, come on. I really think we have to discuss things between us because this is very weird living with you, doing what we did."

"Fucking like wild animals in a man-made cage?"

Pushing her tongue into her cheek, Drew looks at me like the memory has her fired up again. She sighs and adjusts her blouse. "Yes, that."

With my eyes dropping to take her in, I growl, "It was hot."

"It was very hot. And it's not going to go anywhere."

I already know this, but that she's saying it, irks me. I know full well why it has to stop, and why Denver isn't an altogether bad thing when it comes to Drew and keeping my hands off her. I've never had a desire to really love someone, and give them everything. That's not going to change now.

But why is *she* putting the brakes on?

That's what's got me irritated.

"Why not?" I'm expecting her to bring up my age again. I really don't want to hear that shit again. What does age matter? That's not our problem.

"Why not?" she repeats like the answer is obvious.

"Yeah, tell me why."

After a long sigh, she crosses her arms, too. "Do you want something serious? Do you want to be in a relationship?"

Struck silent, I stare at her and finally admit, "No."

Unblinking, we hold each other's look before she slowly nods. "That's what I thought."

"Why does it have to be serious?"

"Because it does. Because it is," she sighs, releasing her arms to run her fingers through her long hair. I can still remember how it smelled when I buried my face in her neck, and I want to smell it again. "Sex is the most intimate thing two people can do together outside of giving birth and killing one another. Acting like it's casual is lying to yourself."

"Lots of people have casual sex and are just fine with that," I argue.

"Not me," she whispers. "I can't do that. After I left today, I drove around the city and I went to Piedmont Park and just sat and thought about things. Today was incredible, Jake. Too incredible. And that's how I know I can't keep sticking my hand in the basket thinking the cobra won't bite. Sooner or later."

"Are you calling my cock a cobra? I'm thinking more python."

She smiles. "I'm being serious."

"I know. I really do agree with you, I just don't like it."

"Me neither." She runs her hands through her hair again and shakes it out. "I will fall for you, if we continue to do what we did today."

"Fuck like our lives depended on it?"

She smiles. "You're ridiculous."

I mutter, pretending to be having fun, "You like it," but there's no smile in my gut or on my face. Losing the jokes, I look at the floor and confess, "I'm not used to this, what you're doing right now. I'm used to games and attempts to manipulate me."

Drew laughs a little. "I'm sure. But isn't it better this way?"

"Harder to hear. You have to face it." I inhale and push off the wall, shoving my hands in my pockets. "You got the job."

Her eyes go wide and her jaw drops open with happy surprise. "I did?"

"Your interview was spectacular. That's what I told my uncle."

She runs over and smacks my arm. "Shut up! Are you fucking with me? I really got the job?"

The fact that she's swearing more lately, I proudly take responsibility for. Smiling I tell her, "Yeah. I told him you were eager."

She hits me again and I can't help but laugh.

"Jake!!!"

"To learn! Eager to learn! No, seriously. You got the job. Congratulations."

Her smile disappears in an instant. "Is it just because we..."

"No! No, I think you'll do great." My mind is on the books she's been studying, but I can't tell her how impressed I am by how she's going after this. The job search was one thing, I knew how hard she was beating the pavement, but that nightly studying really deepens my respect for her.

"My uncle has a thing for helping people, so it was actually in your favor that you have no experience. That's why I have to go to Denver. He kept trying to give this guy Dwight a chance, but he blew it. My uncle thinks he'll still get his shit together and get sober. I'll be there until that happens, I guess." Drew is watching me intently. "Uncle Don never gives up on someone until he has no other choice."

She softly says, "Your uncle sounds like a good man."

"He is." A lump forms in my throat. Now is the perfect time to exit this difficult conversation. "I'll leave you to whatever it is you do at night."

Drew calls after me, "Thank you for the job, Jake. I won't let you guys down."

I wave over my shoulder without looking back. In my room I close my door and take a half dozen deep breaths. Blinking around, I walk to a photo of my own, one that hangs on the wall. It's my brothers and me when I was only fifteen. We're all such different heights here. Jaxson is the oldest but Jett, one year younger is taller than him in this, stockier, too. Jett's got the exact coloring of our father, dirty blonde hair, green eyes—one of the reasons it's so hard for Dad to accept the disparity in their personalities. Jett was named after Dad's father, Jerald. But he dropped that name as soon as he could. Never suited him.

He and Jaxson are the same height now, maybe an inch difference. Jett's still stockier. Jax is sinewy from workin' on his ranch, and he's got a mix of Dad and Mom in him. Emerald green eyes, darker, sandy-brown hair that's a shade lighter than hers and mine. And Jeremy's.

Then there're the twins on either side of me. As tow-headed as they are today, only here they're much skinnier with puberty taking over. Justin's mouth is open because he's telling our mom how to take the picture. Jason is laughing because Justin's bossing her around. I'm smirking because of the shit we pulled that day that Mom didn't know about. I forget what it was, but we got into some kind of trouble in Cascade Springs Park.

In this, I'm scrawnier than the older four, shorter by a couple inches at least. Then there's Jeremy, Mr. Serious, only thirteen, the baby.

"Can't believe you're a Marine now, you fucker," I mutter to his goofy smile. I haven't seen him smile like this in a long time, always so somber now that he's a man.

Grabbing the doorknob, I walk out to find Drew. Her bedroom door is closed, so I knock on it, feeling another tinge of guilt for having broken her privacy earlier. I hear her padding toward me. She opens the door with raised eyebrows, blue eyes guarded.

"Yes?"

"You hungry?"

She pauses. "Actually, yes. Very."

"Let's make some dinner. Watch a movie. Just friends."

She stares at me like she's trying to figure out if I'm tricking her. "Okaaaaay."

I hit the nearest wall and flip around, calling over my shoulder, "Great."

13
DREW

Breakfast for dinner is one of my favorites. When I suggested it, he told me he feels that way, too. Then he tore off his shirt and tossed it onto the floor, explaining he prefers to be shirtless when he's home.

"I noticed," I smiled.

Now we're easily moving around each other while he sautés spinach, ham and onions for omelets, and I fry up red potatoes with some fresh garlic, basil, salt and cracked pepper.

"Bummer we don't have any bacon," I tell him as I add a little more salt.

"Mmmm. Bacon," he mutters. "Did you go to college?"

"This is not something I'm proud of, but no."

Jake flips the sizzling contents of his pan as he says, "I didn't either. But I knew I was staying in construction. Everything I learned was on the job. Been working with Uncle Don since I was fifteen."

Reaching around him, I slide open the utensil drawer to grab a spatula. My arm brushes his naked lower back and electricity sparks. Jake glances at me as I retract my arm and turn over the potatoes. "Ten years at your job and you're only twenty-five? Do you still love it?"

He makes a face like that's a crazy question. "Fuck yeah! That's what men are meant to do. It charges up my battery!" His gaze drops to my pan. "You're turning over every single one of those?"

I nod, carefully poking each potato wedge until it rolls onto its soft side. "I like them to be evenly crisp."

I sneak a look at Jake and catch him smirking at me. A flush fills my cheeks and he laughs, shakes his head and places his pan on a dead burner. Cracking eggs into a fresh one, he hums to himself.

We cook the rest of the meal in an easy silence. Without asking what the other wants to do in terms of duties, I set the table while he pours the orange juice. I turn on some music. He piles food onto our plates. I butter the toast. He takes them from me and places them next to the omelets, says, "I've got it," and carries both of our plates to the dining table.

"Delicious," I finally manage to say after several devoured bites. I didn't realize I was so hungry, but this roommate of mine definitely worked up my appetite earlier. It's hard to keep the images of him groaning in

COCKY ROOMIE: JAKE COCKER

ecstasy away as he sits across from me here, a mere hours later.

Friends.

How am I going to be just friends with this man?

"When was the last time you talked to your husband?"

I wince because it's unexpectedly difficult to hear that title after what I did today. "He called a couple nights ago."

Jake's fork freezes as his eyes meet mine rather violently. "He did? What'd he want?"

I shrug it off. "Wanted to ask if I'd just give him the house outright since he earned the money to pay for it."

"Fucking prick."

I stare at Jake, because he literally growled that. Pushing my food around, I agree, "Yeah. Edward wasn't always that way, though."

"Yeah, he was."

"What do you mean?" I squirm because this subject is still too painful. He must sense that, because he goes back to eating, taking a couple slower bites before he changes the subject. "You ever been to the Botanical Gardens?"

Stabbing a couple potato wedges onto my fork, I offer, "I parked there today to go to Piedmont Park."

"Yeah, that's what made me think of it. Ever been?" I shake my head. "Let's go tomorrow after work. I think you'd like it, Drew."

He goes back to eating like the invitation was nothing. It sounds like a date.

What's he playing at?

I watch him eat as if nothing is amiss. After a couple bites, I softly concede, "Okay."

"You want to carpool to work?" He glances up as he's about to drink some orange juice. "It's not a hard question."

I smile, "Sure. Yeah. That'd be great."

He nods, takes a sip, then asks like it's nothing, "Was your husband the only other guy you've been with?"

I drop my fork, and wipe my mouth with a napkin. "Why would you think that?"

Did my voice actually just crack? Really? Come on!

"You married at nineteen," he says frankly, leaning back with toast in his hand. He takes a huge bite of it, face totally casual.

"I could have slept with other boys in high school."

"Did you?" he asks, chewing. His eyes betray him. They're on fire with curiosity.

I pick my fork up, appetite vanishing as I keep my eyes down to answer, "I've only been with Edward."

"Until today."

Lightning cracks in my veins. Jake has a funny way of bringing this out in me. I'm on edge often, and sometimes I like it. But not right now.

Slowly I lay my fork down. "Yes."

We can't look away from each other. He sets his fork down, too, and leans forward to rest his elbows on the table. Under his steady gaze my heart starts pounding in all kinds of unusual places. What does he want me to say? That I want him? I do, God help me. But I will not sacrifice my sanity.

I hold my breath, waiting for another question that will strip the ability to digest this delicious food we had so much fun making. At least, I had fun. Was it just a game for him?

Stormy brown eyes are tense with determination to keep his hands off me, or *on* me, and I can't tell which!

Frankly, I am not sure what I'd do if he made a move. We tore down the boundary of never having touched today. Putting it mildly.

Would I have the courage to turn him away?

"Drew..."

"Mmm?"

"I want to throw this table to the ground and pin you to this wall." He clenches his jaw. "It's taking all I have to resist the urge of making you beg me again. I know I could do it."

"Well, that's very assumptive of you."

"I know I could do it. But I respect you, and I respect what you're trying to do. Starting your life up. A real life. Of your own." He pauses, the struggle of his evolved self competing with his primal, baser one. It's riveting to watch. "I think it's wrong that you've waited this long to work for yourself, have your own place, be in a city that has so much to offer you. I'm glad you went to the park today. I'm glad my Uncle gives people with empty resumes a chance. I don't know what's going to happen to you. You may not like it here after a while. You may move back. You may become Mayor one day, who knows?"

I laugh softly at the idea. "Oh please, I'm not going to be..."

"You have no idea what you're going to be, Drew." He holds my look with meaning. "You're only just now trying to find out."

My smile vanishes, ache in my chest too strong. "Thank you, Jake. That's very nice of you to say."

"I don't know how much more time I have before I go to Denver, but I need *you* to know this. You're right. The main reason I won't be stripping you naked every day until I leave, isn't because I wasn't planning on anything serious, and you want serious. It's because I really respect what you're doing, and I don't want to confuse you. If I continued to fuck you the way I want to fuck you—and today was only a taste of that —it would make my leaving very hard for you to concentrate."

"You're a cocky asshole, Jake. I would be able to concentrate."

"So, you want me to turn this table over and shred those clothes, and your sweet-tasting, tight little cunt with them?"

A spark snaps to attention. "No. I do not want that."

"You're lying. But that just makes it easier for me to keep my word. I won't try fucking you again before I leave. I can't make any promises for when I return." He rises up, abs flexing as he reaches over and grabs my plate. "You done with this?"

"I've lost my appetite."

"For food." He lays one plate on the other, picks up my toast, puts it in his mouth, grabs the silverware and heads off. I watch his perfect ass until he disappears into the kitchen, thinking, *my hands gripped onto that today, only it was naked then.*

My body is on fire and I'm confused. Blinking around me, I have no idea what to do with myself. He may be the most obnoxiously confident man I've ever met when it comes to the awareness of his sexual skills, but he's right about his abilities. One-hundred-twenty-percent on the money.

He felt so good.

So right.

He's also correct about how it would affect me. I can barely concentrate now and I'm only *thinking* about sex.

Screw it. He can clean up the orange juice glasses. I'm going to bed...and to my vibrator.

"Goodnight," I call to the kitchen.

"Night, Drew. Lock your door."

Lock my door? Is it really that hard for him to resist me? That he wants me this badly is beyond wonderful. I don't want to go to bed alone.

Holding my breath, I stand still in the beginning of the short hallway that leads to my room.

By not disappearing just yet, I'm tempting me, him,

and fate. Caution and reason have flown out the window.

Walk out here, Jake. Come out of the kitchen and see me standing here offering myself. If you do, I won't turn you away. I'm waiting. Walk out and see me unbuttoning my blouse.

The kitchen faucet turns on and I hear the clattering of pans collected. He's going to clean up our mess. He always does the dishes right after cooking. It's one of the most shocking things about him, considering his age and brutish ways.

Unfortunately for us, it will be some time before he is done. Just long enough for me to second-think this invitation.

Shutting myself into the safety of my bedroom, it takes a long time for me to actually turn the lock. When I do, my eyes close and I rest a pained frown against the cool wood door.

I wish he'd break it down.

I wouldn't turn him away.

But he knows that.

14

JAKE

"*M*orning," Drew mutters, as she appears in the kitchen.

From where I'm watching fresh coffee brew, I glance back and give her the once over. "Nice dress."

She looks down and touches the belt. "Thank you. I bought some clothes for work if I ever got a job." A shy smile appears and she fingers a tiny locket around her neck. I linger on it, wondering if her husband's picture is inside.

I'm not going to ask.

Not yet. Maybe not ever.

Even though now it's all I can think about.

I slept like shit last night. Dreamt of Drew spread out on my desk, touching herself and moaning. Only my office was outside at the job site and there were a bunch of my colleagues ogling her. I woke up hard as a rock and ready to fight at the same time. Fucking frustrating bullshit. But I meant what I said. I want her focused on setting her foundation. I know from being an expert in construction that without one, whatever else you build will come falling down with the first thunderstorm. And life is full of them.

"Milk?" she asks, opening the fridge and holding up a carton.

I nod as I pour coffee into two thermoses for the first time. "How'd you sleep, Drew?"

"Not well," she whispers, pouring the cold, white liquid. We share a knowing glance. "You didn't either huh?" she smiles.

"Nah." I twist the lids into place, hand hers over and walk to my shoes. "I'll keep my promise though."

"What promise?" She picks up her purse and slides the strap onto her shoulder.

"To keep my hands off you until I get back from Denver," I smirk. "You just wanted to hear me say it again, didn't you?" I pick up my keys.

She smiles, "Maybe," slipping into her heels. She's looking down to put them on, and her long hair falls softly in front of her face. She tucks some behind her ear so she can glance over to me and read my expression. She's so fucking beautiful as she does this simple little gesture, and she has no idea how badly I want to touch her.

This is going to be a bitch and a half.

"You're saying you want to date when you get back?" she asks with a look that kills me.

"No. I'm saying I'll...never mind. I don't want to talk about it." Holding the door open for her, I grate, "I don't know when I'm coming back, but if you're still single when I do, I know I will fuck you again."

A shocked laugh escapes her and she walks by me, hesitating as our arms brush against each other. Our eyes meet and she says, simply, "You're really full of yourself."

I chuckle, "Better than being a fucking, insecure pussy."

&.

*T*he office is a lot more interesting with her in it. I feel more awake than I have here in a long time, and I'm not the only one. Uncle Don is peacocking for Drew since she's soaking everything he says in like he's her favorite professor in a college she didn't think would accept her. Eager to learn *and* pretty to look at—that's an inspiring tonic for any heterosexual man.

Juan, Diego, Evan and Hank are all hanging around longer than they normally would, too.

"Alright, enough questions," I grumble to the group lingering around the front desk. "She's got a lot to learn and I don't have enough time to teach her."

"You could teach me, Jake, and then I'll take over when you're gone," Hank smiles to Drew who instantly blushes. That sets me off. I'm the only one she blushes for, goddammit.

"Yeah, Hank, because you and math go hand in

hand. Blind leading the blind. Don't you have a tank that needs emptying?"

He chuckles and hits Evan on the shoulder then eyes me with a knowing smirk. Letting a guy like him know I'm interested in Drew is like lighting a match at a gas station. His voice lowers. "Don't need to know math to show a woman a good time."

Embarrassed, Drew's eyes are cast down to her lap.

I'm about to punch him when my uncle barks, "Hank! That's sexual harassment and I won't have it here. You got me?"

The guys back off, everyone awkward.

Hank grits his teeth and puffs his chest at Uncle Don. The workers file out to drive to today's site. They won't be back until the end of day, if at all. That's a good thing.

The air is tight, and I'm about to ask Drew if she's okay, when my Uncle says, "Jake, I booked you a flight for Tuesday."

Drew and I both stare at him in silence as my throat dries up. "That soon?"

He nods his answer, laying down a three-ring binder in front of Drew. "Read through our company policies for me, Mrs. Charles, while I speak to my nephew a minute."

She nods as he motions for me to follow him.

In his office, I shut the door and say with a lot more anger than I'd planned, "You're going to watch over Hank when I'm gone? I don't like how he looked at her."

Uncle Don sits on his desk and levels me with a wise look. "Hank was just riling you up."

"No, he can spot a prize when he sees one. And he's a sexist fuck who needs a beating," I growl.

"Uh-huh. Do you have any idea how much you were staring at that poor woman, Jake?"

My frown deepens and I shove my hands into my pockets. "I wasn't staring at her."

My uncle chuckles and shakes his head. "Okay. Sure. But yeah, you were. You have something you want to tell me?"

"Like what?" I shrug.

"You ask her out? That fight you two had, was it a lover's quarrel? What? Fess up."

I cross my arms. "We're...friends. That's it."

"You like that girl."

"She's not a girl. She's eight years older than me."

He whistles under his breath. "Hot."

I can't help but smile, "Dude."

He chuckles while flipping on his computer. "Older women, younger men, it's the new thing. I read what's on the internet."

"I see what you're doing, but I don't do relationships, Uncle Don, you know that."

"Who said you have to?" He winks at me.

Anger rises from my gut without warning and I shoot him a look. "Don't talk about her like Hank did. She deserves to be happy. I can't make her happy."

I walk out without looking back.

15

DREW

*J*ake is quiet on the ride home. He was very professional with me today, after he came to my rescue when the men swarmed around. But after he spoke to his uncle, he treated me like I was just a co-worker. I'm sure he's got Denver on his mind. That's going to be a big change for him.

Still, I would have liked to catch him stealing a glance at me at least once. I know that's selfish, but all day I couldn't get him out of my mind for long. Thank God I was learning all new things or I would have been a wreck.

He leaves Tuesday.

That's too soon.

Part of me wishes it were sooner.

My heart is saying time doesn't matter, there is something special here. And my mind thinks I'm just ruining the first chance I have at making a childhood dream come true.

Marietta Street flies by the window. It's Friday now. Tuesday is just around the corner. He's moving away and I'll live in his home all by myself.

What a lonely nightmare.

"Your uncle was nice for sticking up for me today."

Jake's thick hands tighten on the steering wheel. He gives a curt nod. "Watch out for Hank when I'm gone."

"Okay."

Storefronts blur past our silence. We're almost home when his knuckles regain their color and he reaches over to lay his hand on my thigh. The warmth from his palm is both soothing and jarring but I hope he keeps it there. Feeling him watching me, I glance over to meet his troubled gaze. "If Hank gives you any trouble, will you tell me?"

"Sure."

"I'll have my brothers take care of it." He's dead serious.

"Okay."

He nods and leaves an empty feeling behind as both hands grip the wheel hard. "Botanical gardens tonight."

"Really?"

"Yeah," he mutters. "May as well make the most of the few days I've got left here. With my *friend* Drew." He huffs through his nose.

"You *really* don't want to go to Denver, do you?"

"Not at all. I've never been there. I'm sure it's fine."

He makes the last turn onto our street. "I'm just going to miss my family, that's all. And my city."

I touch his thigh, too, wanting to comfort him. "I'm sorry, Jake." He relaxes and exhales.

"Me too." Pulling into the parking lot, he leans forward in concentration and breaks into a grin. "Oh shit!" Cutting a mischievous smirk to me, he puts his hand over mine. "Ready to meet my brothers?"

❧

*A*s soon as Jake opens our front door, we are ambushed. I'd been warned they had a key and would be waiting inside, but I never expected how different they would look from him.

"What the fuck, Jake?!!

"When were you gonna tell us you're fuckin' leaving, man?"

Jake exhales, "Dad called you."

Since they're focused on Jake, I have a chance to study them a little. The blonde, green-eyed twins are a couple inches taller than their brother. All three men are exquisitely well built, but Jake is stockier and they are sinewy. It's like the difference between football players and soccer players.

The one dressed in an expensive suit says, "Yeah, he fuckin' called us. He called everyone. Have you checked your phone, you piece of shit?" He grabs Jake and bear hugs him, closing his eyes.

I take a step back to give the brothers room, feeling like I'm seeing something not meant for me.

Pulling away, Jake asks, "He called Jett?"

The twins shake their heads, and the air gets heavier, making me curious when they both say, "Nah. Not him."

Jake nods.

The Suit changes the subject by focusing on me to offer his hand. "I'm Justin." We shake and he holds onto my hand. "You must be Drew, our brother's new hot babe roommate."

A blush creeps up as I glance to Jake.

Is that how he described me?

"Nice to meet you, Justin."

Jake smirks, "Let go of her hand, Justin."

That means the other twin is the one Jake mentioned was a music producer, mostly of Hip Hop. Dressed in casual, stylish clothes fitting for that industry, he's got a baseball hat on, and it's backward. He holds out his hand as he sizes me up. He grins, "Jason. I'm sure you've heard all about me. So, how is it living with this guy, huh?" He looks at Jake and winks.

"How many times do I have to tell you assholes to take your shoes off in my home?"

"She's pretty, Jake."

"No wonder why you left us high and dry at The Vortex the other night."

Jake laughs, "Shut up."

Jason bumps his shoulder to Justin's. "He didn't say she had a rack on her, either."

My jaw drops as I make a shocked sound.

"Alright, no looking at my roommate's tits."

"Thank you," I tell him.

He smirks at me. "That's my job."

"Oh my God!" I scream. "You are all truly unbelievable."

I cover my chest with tightly crossed arms, and they're all smiling the same smile. Three gorgeous men trained on me. I just might faint.

"No good, Drew," Justin says. "That only hikes the beauties up. Why don't girls know this?"

I cry out, "Stop it!" and go to leave because I'm the color of a radish, but the three of them block my way.

Jake grabs me, lifts me up and spins me around, putting me right back where I was. "Ah ah ah...not so fast." He turns to the twins. "Since everyone's still got their fucking shoes on, *morons,* you wanna go to the Botanical Gardens with us?"

"Shit yes," Jason mutters, hitting his pockets for his keys. He disappears into the living room. And apparently cute butts run in the family.

Justin slides his hands into his slack's pockets, pushing up the suit jacket a little with the motion. He smirks from me to Jake. "Botanical Gardens? Sounds romantic, Jake. So not like you."

Jake counters with equal ease, "I have a thing for plants."

"Is that what they're calling them these days? Ouch! You don't have to hit me!"

Jason runs back to us, opens the front door, and

bows so deeply and theatrically that his baseball hat falls off. He catches it with one hand, flips it around and puts it back on with a flourish. "My lady! After you."

Now I understand what the women of Atlanta must have been aware of long before I arrived...

The Cocker Brothers are *dangerous*.

16

JAKE

*J*ustin challenges Jason, "I dare you," after Jason threatens to walk into Cascade Garden's fountain. "Do it. What are they going to do, throw us out?"

Jason smiles, "You mean *again*?" hanging a foot over the water.

Grinning, I glance to Drew. She really doesn't

want to be thrown out. She already whispered to me that she'll return often while I'm gone. I bought her a membership, but she didn't see me do it. She just thought it was a normal ticket. Twenty-one dollars for one visit versus seventy-five for year round? Easy decision.

To put her out of her misery, I start walking away so she'll follow my lead. She quickly catches up with me. Jason and Justin are razzing each other behind us with the latter calling the former a pussy for not going in. You don't have to make a big deal about asking people to stop acting like assholes. All you have to do is walk away and act like something else is more interesting. They lose the audience and get the hint.

"So, you like it?" I ask her as we stroll along the green path.

"It's beautiful! I've never seen anything like it."

Stealing a glance from the corner of my eyes, I catch her drinking in the wildflowers and ferns on the forest floor. "Where are you from again?"

"Dublin, a couple hours south of here." She glances to me and looks quickly at the trees. "I can see what you're thinkin'. And yes, I've had a sheltered life. Haven't been many places. We went to Savannah for vacations because of the beach nearby. And Charleston, too. Edward wasn't a fan of bigger cities, though. Too many people for him." She shrugs and meets my eyes. "I think he was afraid of losin' me, too. I like people. I love festivals. I like the energy and the diversity. I always wanted to live here, but it wasn't an option."

"Why didn't you speak up to him? Tell him what you wanted?"

She stares ahead as we approach the Kendeda Canopy Walk, and her steps hesitate at my tone. Her voice grows quieter as she asks, "You think I'm weak, don't you? I did speak up, sometimes, but...I guess when you've grown up with somethin' it just becomes the way things are. Like you're trained. I was used to him leadin'" She frowns and shakes her head. "It's not fun havin' regrets, Jake. Don't let that happen to you."

"I go after what I want." We're quiet for a bit, and it occurs to me that I've sunk the mood with my questions. It just feels like I've got no time and I want to know more about her. Shallow chit chat isn't my strong suit anyway. But I don't like her frowning like that. Clearing my throat I offer, "Sounds like this divorce is the best thing that could have happened to you."

Drew looks at me with a thoughtful expression. A beautiful smile lights her up, and she nods.

"You are getting a divorce, right?"

"Yes! Are you kiddin'? Absolutely."

"I didn't know if you were going to be one of the couples who never actually files the papers."

Drew stops walking and holds my gaze. "I'm getting divorced. Debra Morales will make sure Edward serves me those papers. Are you askin' because..." She pauses as a drop of water splashes her nose. We both look up as she wipes it away, more rain-drops taking its place, falling on both of us now.

When it rains in Georgia, it doesn't send you an invitation. It just arrives.

Behind me Justin strolls up smirking, "Didn't even see those clouds come in, did ya? Little distracted?"

I shoot him a look. "You're gonna mess up your suit, Jus. What's your maid gonna think when she sees it crumpled up on the floor."

"Just another day in the Cocker Penthouse," he smirks.

Jogging over, Jason chuckles, "You set that right up, Jake. And he just knocked it down." He's got a fucking Hydrangea flower in his hand, branch stem slivered from where he busted it. "For the lady," he smiles as the rain picks up.

Drew happily accepts the gift, glancing to me like the thing is amazing. She'd pointed out how much she liked them earlier, when we first got here. Jason, romantic, charming bastard that he is, took note.

As she slowly turns it, raindrops gather on the groups of tiny petals and in her sweet-smelling hair.

I share a look with my brother, one Drew doesn't see. He realizes I am not pleased he made me look bad here.

I should have given her that flower.

Justin is smiling between us with a *Jason-you're-such-a-dumb-shit* look. Behind that is a smirk that adds, *Jake, you're not telling us everything...but we know.*

I place my hand on Drew's back to guide her. "Let's keep walking. It's about to come down hard."

Under her breath she says, "I hope there's gonna be lightnin'."

The four of us find protection beneath an underpass. The gardens are vast with paths in every direction. We'll stay here until the downpour lightens.

Up to no good, as usual, Justin asks, "Hey Drew, what do you do for a living?" Before she has a chance to give them more kindling to blast me with, Justin's phone goes off. "It's Dad," he tells us, walking away with rain pounding in the background. Jason joins him; the maneuver anything but subtle.

Drew is staring at the rain with a strange look on her face. "What are you thinking about?"

Quiet enough that they can't hear, and with the heavy downpour helping, she privately says, "I saw you didn't want to tell them where I work."

"They're just fucking with me. It's what brothers do. I didn't want to deal with it."

She nods. "It isn't because I fucked you to get the job?" A sneaky smile lights her eyes.

Taken off guard, a guffaw breaks free from my lungs. "Drew, sometimes you're as delicate as that flower, and other times, watch out!"

Jason and Justin look over, curious, amused.

She's grinning as she removes a small leaf from my shirt, then whispers, "You bring it out in me, Jake."

My cock twitches. Suddenly I wish I hadn't asked

them to come with us. This tunnel in the rainstorm would be the perfect place for a hot kiss.

Returning, Justin's voice rises to provoke me with, "Dad, tell Mom we're *bringing a guest* to the BBQ."

My eyes flash over.

He's grinning like the Devil would after signing a pact with a virgin, "Yeah, it's Jake's new roommate. Uncle Don just hired her." Now how the fuck did he know that? Asshole. He pauses as the tunnel lights up then explodes with a thunderclap. "We're at the Botanical Gardens with her now. Nice girl. Alright, Dad. We'll see you Sunday night. Bye." Justin slides the phone into his pocket. "Well, look at what I did."

Jason changes his hat so the bill is in front, then he dips his head to hide a grin behind it.

Having someone to a Family BBQ would be a first for me. He knows this. I've never brought anyone to one of these things, neither has he! And this particular one is even more family-only because it's a goodbye send-off. But I'm stuck between a rock and a stone, so I force a smile. "You're going to love my Mom's fresh ginger ale."

From her expression, she knows I'm not happy about this.

We all look over as the rain does what it's famous for in the South—leaves as quickly as it came. Quarter-sized raindrops are replaced with dimes, then drizzle. We're all used to it, so no one mentions it. We just wait for it to do its thing.

Justin and Jason head out first.

Drew hangs back and grabs my wrist as I go to follow. "Jake, I'm not goin' to the BBQ."

"You have plans?"

"No, I just don't want to go."

I frown, surprised. Since when does a girl you had sex with turn down meeting your family? Especially when you're a fucking Cocker. I can't even count how many have tried to come over to my parents house before.

"Why not? Not many people get invited. It's kind of a big deal."

Off my defensiveness, she smiles a little and shakes her head. "Jake, that's *not* why I'm not goin'. It's just, you're about to leave. For who knows how long. This'll be the last chance to spend time with your family. You don't need an outsider there. The focus will be on me, and it should be on you. With everyone comfortable."

I'm stunned speechless. For years my brothers and I have deflected girls and their Mommas who try to snake into our tight-knit clan. Most do it for the wrong reasons, so we're careful. Our family comes from money. Our dad is a Congressman. We're not bad looking. That equals targets on our backs.

And here Drew is looking out for *my* best interests?

"Huh," I mutter.

"Let's go." She walks away, glancing over her shoulder to see if I'm coming. "Come on."

I follow her out and when she pauses to let me catch up, I walk in silence beside her, processing this. Finally I mumble, "You're a good person."

She cuts a quick look to me. "You too."

"I don't know about that."

"Just take a fuckin' compliment."

I burst out laughing. "Cuss words coming out of your mouth always surprise me."

"I'm not a priss!"

Remembering my face in her sweet, hot, wet little cunt, I smirk to myself. "Oh, I know."

When we catch up to my brothers, Jason announces plans to go to Whiskey Mistress, a bar in Buckhead where he's hot for one of the bartenders. The invitation is meant for everyone present, but Drew declines and gives me a look meant for only me to understand. We drive her home then head north without her.

I'm relieved when they leave the subject of my roommate alone for most of the night. But after more than a few samplings of the various high-end bourbons on the back wall, Justin nearly shouts, "So, have you fucked her yet?"

My bourbon goes everywhere.

They lose it laughing.

The bartender of Jason's current sexual focus strolls over to clean up my reaction with a damp towel. "Did you have to spit all over my new cardboard coasters?"

"Sorry, Jenny." With the back of my hand I wipe off my lips. "Justin's got the delicacy of a rhino."

"From the spit-take, I'd say that's a YES."

"No. It's a no. I haven't touched her."

Honestly surprised, Jason cuts in to demand, "What? Why not!?"

I'm a good liar.

Justin announces way too loudly, "If it were me, I'd be hitting that every night and not coming up for air until she begged me for sleep."

I glare at him. "Stop thinking about that."

"You can't control what I think, Jake. What? I can't *think* about fucking your roommate?" He leans in, daring me to punch him.

I growl, "No, you fucking can't," leaning toward him. "So just get it out of your head!"

He holds my look and for a second I think it's on. But then he smacks my shoulder in a friendly way and leans back, grinning over to his twin. "See, Jason? I told you! He likes her. God, you're so easy to play, Jake, you know that?"

I glare at him, mutter, "Fuck you" and cut a glance to Jenny as she sets down a new drink for me. "Thanks."

"No problem. Try to drink that one, 'kay?" She smiles from me to Jason where she pauses a long moment before helping her other customers.

Irritated, I rake my eyes over the glittering Atlanta skyline. It's a nice night, so it's packed out there on the patio. We prefer sitting at the bar. Especially when Jason is banging the girl behind it.

Jason says, "You like her, Jake," appearing serious, but who the fuck knows, right? He could be setting me up. "Why aren't you doing anything about it?"

"I'm not falling into this trap again. You're not going to get a rise out of me again tonight, so let's just change the subject."

"I'm really asking, Jake."

I exhale and stare at him before I shrug, "She wants different things. And she's eight years older."

"Hot," Justin mutters. "Why do you have a problem with that? Younger girls can be a pain in the ass."

I huff, "The age difference doesn't bother me, Justin, but it bothers her."

He informs me, "Tell her Susan Sarandon was eight years older than Tim Robbins."

"Didn't last," Jason reminds him.

"It lasted like fifteen years," I say.

"Twenty, I think," Justin says, then thinks about it. "Something like that. Then she dated some guy thirty years younger than her."

"Total fucking douche," Jason mutters.

"And Goldie Hawn and Kurt Russell!" Justin says, poking my chest. "Tell her about them. She's eight years older. They're still together."

"Tina Turner and that guy...can't remember his name," Jason says, thinking. "Sixteen years older. *And* they look happy."

Justin leans in again, this time as serious as his twin. "The list goes on and on. I'm just saying, you like her. She's a sweetheart. It doesn't have to be forever. Show her some things. I guarantee she'll thank you for it."

Jason mutters, "Jesus, you're an asshole."

"What?" Justin asks him. "That girl blushes. She fucking *blushes*. She hasn't seen her way around the right bed. Is she a virgin or what the hell?"

"Married," I mutter. "One guy."

"And she's thirty-one?"

"You don't know how old I am? Or did you forget how to count?"

"Whatever. Thirty-three. Only one guy her whole life. This is what I'm saying, she needs to learn what it's all about." He pauses, thinking, and starts laughing.

Jason and I look at him and demand at the same time, "What?!"

"If that's what she needs, she's rented the right room." He downs his whiskey and sets the empty glass down.

Before calling Jenny over, Jason says to me, "If you don't do it, I'm sure Justin will. Hey, beautiful! Can I have another?"

"You got it, handsome," Jenny calls back.

With my eyes locked on Justin's, I tell him firmly, "Don't even think about it, Jus. I'm not kidding."

He chuckles. "Better make a move, Jake. Just sayin'."

"You better be fucking with me right now."

"I probably am."

"Probably?"

"Yep."

I glare at him. Jenny interrupts just in time to see

me jump off my barstool so fast it falls over. "I'm outta here. Jenny, *Justin's* buying."

Jason calls after me, "You're not driving like this!"

"I'm takin' a Lyft," I shout, pushing everyone out of my way.

I didn't even realize I fell asleep until I'm awoken by the sound of the front door. I groggily pick up my phone for the time. Two twenty-two. From the sound of his gait, he and the twins had more than a few. Did he drive home? Is he walking toward my room?

He is.

Clumsy footsteps stop right outside my door. I'm frozen. Not breathing. Craning my head, I discover that I didn't lock the door. Is he going to come in here?

"Drew," he rasps through the wood. "You up?"

Stay quiet. Don't answer him. You won't be able to turn him away if you answer him.

If he comes in that door, I will give him anything he wants. Even if he is five sheets to the wind. I might want to brush my teeth first, but I will let him in. Everywhere.

"Drew?"

I hold my breath, staring at the doorknob, my pussy starting to pulse.

Suspenseful moments tick by. Finally he trudges away. Sitting up in bed, my heart pounds as I listen to him go about his nightly routine until the door of his own bedroom shuts. I've memorized the sound. I've tried not to, but when he's home I'm very aware of his every move. It's unhealthy.

I'm becoming relieved he's going to Denver. I can't take this abstinence for much longer. I'm terrible at it! And at the same time, I'm going to miss him very much.

Seeing him interacting with his brothers didn't help. He was so at ease around them, so himself without any guards up. Laughing often. Cracking jokes at each other's expense. Having so much fun it made me wish even more that I'd been born into a larger family. And that I'd had one of my own. There was such friendship between the three of them, such love even though they hid it behind sarcasm. I could have spent the whole day with them, it was so much fun.

I'd turned down joining them at the bar for the same reason I blocked the unwanted invite to his family's goodbye party. My being present was a distraction, and they wouldn't see each other for who knows how long! Men need their time alone, especially brothers, I would imagine. I'm sure they didn't come over here expecting me, a stranger, to tag along now that they'd discovered Jake was moving away, and so quickly, too! They'd come to see him, spend time with him, show him they're going to miss him in the masculine way that they do.

Family.

My head sinks into the pillow as I think about what I lost, and what Debra has gained.

Although I wouldn't want it to be with Edward, I know now. Having children with him would have been an un-escapable life sentence. At least I'm free, even if I am childless.

Throwing the covers off, I head to the bathroom. My mouth tastes gross and I have to pee. When I turn on the light, his wet toothbrush says hello to me from the counter. He left it in a puddle of clear water, and his socks are shoved in a corner on the floor. I touch my toes to them and push them around a bit.

Oh, Drew, you are falling hard for this guy if you're thinking of his cute toes while touching these stinky things.

Brushing my teeth is done on automatic with my mind traveling back to the garden paths with him. The way he touched my leg in the car like it was a normal thing to do. Him pouring me coffee before we started our workday like we were a couple. Swinging me around when I tried to escape his brother's embarrassing comments about my chest.

Who am I kidding?

I don't want him to leave.

I want him to stay.

Staring at my reflection I shake my head and lay my toothbrush down, spitting and rinsing quickly while I turn off the water and finally give a resigned sigh.

Opening the bathroom door, I run smack into Jake.

"Oh! God, you scared me."

Of course he's wearing no shirt. But black boxer-briefs? Really? Is he trying to kill me?

He rasps, "Hey," his voice filled with sex.

Oh. Fuck.

"Umm...hey?"

His gorgeous features darken, eyes grazing my lips. "You still against casual sex?"

"Oh my God. Yes, Jake, I am."

I can smell the minty toothpaste on his breath. I guess he can smell mine, too. Especially leaning in this close. I go to back up, but he reaches around me and closes the bathroom door, putting his forearms on it and caging me between them.

"What if the fuck I gave you was so good you didn't mind if we weren't serious about each other?"

Desire for him to come closer lashes through my cells as we stare at each other. "What if pigs turned into giraffes and ate the top of pine trees?"

Jake blinks at me. "That makes no sense."

"Well, you're scramblin' my brains Jake Cocker!!"

For a second it looks like he's going to laugh, but lust replaces humor. "You're scramblin' my everything, Drew Charles." He leans in and brushes his lips up my neck, sending wet flames into my surprised pussy. The fact that he can light me up this fast is a miracle. I used to be slow to get riled, but not with him. He growls in my ear, "I want to lick you until you cum on my tongue."

"Fuck," I whisper, arching my back until we're pressed together. He groans like this is exactly what he needed, too, and buries his face in my neck, gnawing on it in the most sensuously slow fashion. "Jake, remember you said you didn't want me to lose focus."

"Mmmmhmm."

"You promised not to distract me."

"I'm leaving Tuesday. You'll have plenty of time to study then."

I won't be able to think, if I'm missing you! I will ache for you every day, you idiot.

One hand goes around me, and the other slowly palms my breasts over my tank top. His erection presses against me and I moan as he says, "I want to bury my cock in you again."

But this isn't right.

I already feel pain.

I can see the future and it is lonely.

"I can't, Jake. I'm sorry." I push him off. "Please stop." He staggers back and runs both hands through his hair to gain control of himself. My eyes are on the x-rated tent in his black boxer-briefs. I try to bend the door with my body by hiding against it. "I *want* to, but I'm not made that way."

"I know. It's why I like you. And why I hate you, too."

Appalled, I cry out, "Don't say you hate me!"

A few quick strides and Jake is on me. He grabs the

back of my head, slams our mouths together, and kisses me so deeply and so desperately that all of my objections turn to ash in his arms. He lifts me up by my thighs, grinding his angry length against the damp crotch of my pajama shorts. I moan into his mouth as my core responds and softens to him. He sets me violently down and careens away from me, gasping for air.

He's left me panting, staring at him, needing more, and this is when he stops?

"Drew, if I still feel like this when I'm in Denver, I'm going to come back and fucking make you MINE." His eyes violently flash to me. All his muscles have tensed. His restraint is barely winning the war with his primal instincts. "YA HEAR ME?"

Breathless, I whisper, "Yes."

He marches to his room and slams himself inside. "Lock your fucking door AGAIN!" he shouts through the wood.

I'm going to come back and fucking make you mine.

Jake Cocker is second-guessing single life, because of how he feels...about me.

I float to my room, knowing my dreams tonight won't be half as good as my reality.

"Jaxson's here!" Mom calls to everyone in the backyard. My oldest brother appears behind her in his usual country-plaid shirt and faded blue jeans. He picks Mom up and spins her around. Laughing, she hollers at him, "Come on now! You know I get dizzy!"

He plants a kiss on her cheek, sets her down, and strolls onto the patio deck, taking in the strings of lights, long table of net-covered, homemade Nancy Cocker specialties, before finally nodding to all of our familiar faces.

"What's this I hear about Jake leavin' Georgia?!" He calls to the crowd.

Everyone boos and grumbles.

"Blame Don!" our dad shouts with a cupped hand, his deep voice regal even as he goes for the laugh.

Dad's assistant and her husband smile. They're not here often, so they must have made the trip down from

DC to do what was needed so he could stay in town until I leave. Further down the yard, their two kids chase after the neighborhood cat nobody owns but everyone feeds and has a different name for. *We* call him Pippin.

"Alright, alright!" Don yells back, rolling his eyes. "I'm never gonna live this down, am I?"

Jaxson mutters, "No, you are not," his eyes on me as we head for each other.

Aunt Marie tells her husband, "No, Don, you really won't." She wraps her pillowy arm around him and lays her head on his beefy shoulder.

Jaxson and I embrace and I smell the familiar scent of hay and fresh air. He lives on a ranch in northern Georgia, an hour outside the perimeter of Atlanta, so I don't see him as much as the twins. Sometimes I go up and stay the weekend with him just to spend quality time with my eldest brother.

He's a man who doesn't need much. Doesn't like cities. Gets his milk from his cows. Farms his own vegetables which he sells to the local markets and restaurants. And he hasn't had a girlfriend in who the hell knows how long. At least in the city, you can find casual hookups easily. Jaxson living up there means he's practically celibate compared to the rest of us.

I think he's waiting for something, someone. How that person is going to find him all the way out in the quiet country where the nearest house is acres away, I'll never know.

When I'm staying at his home, I live like he does,

up at the asscrack of dawn, and then reading until we can't keep our eyes open, talking on and off, but mostly just enjoying comfortable quiet.

There's a depth to Jax felt anytime you're in his presence, so I know my big brother won't joke about this move. I'm about to have my chest twisted as we separate. He will dig deep.

"How ya feelin' 'bout this?" he asks in his lowest volume, emerald green eyes searching mine with concern.

"Good."

"Don't lie to me."

"Not good."

He nods. "Yeah. We're gonna miss ya. You wanna come up next weekend before you head off?"

"I leave Tuesday."

His frown deepens. A lump builds in my throat as he grabs and hugs me even harder than the first time. We slap shoulders and separate, him shaking his head that it's a damn shame.

"Chili time!" Mom calls out the kitchen window. "Justin, Jason, come help me!"

They both run in. Justin calls over to me as he passes, "Where's Drew?"

"Don't worry about Drew," I tell him. He grins and disappears.

"Who's Drew?" Jaxson asks.

I shrug, "Roommate," not wanting to talk about her.

"What's he like?"

"*She.*"

His eyebrows shoot up. "So that's why Justin's asking about her. You got a hot roommate? That wise?"

"Keep it down. She works for Likuss now and I don't want Uncle Don to hear us talkin' about her."

Jaxson grins, "So, you're in a shit-storm is what you're tellin' me."

"It's nothing I can't handle."

The green in his eyes catches fire. "If Justin's asking about her, she must be memorable."

"If Justin touches her, I'll personally castrate the guy. Blood or no blood."

"Huh," Jaxson mutters, watching me.

Aunt Marie announces, "Jaxson Cocker, give your aunt a hug!" walking up with open arms. She's the female coloring of Dad. The leaf didn't fall far from the tree there, both tall and fair-haired. "I haven't seen you in almost a month!" She squeezes him hard. "How's the farm?"

"Good, Aunt Marie. How's that herb garden coming?"

She waves him away. "Oh please! It's four little pots in my window sill."

"It's a garden in my book," he smiles. "Hey, Uncle Don!"

"How're ya doin' son?" They heartily shake hands.

"It's nothing compared to your garden!" Aunt Marie mutters, smiling.

"Good, good. Workin' hard," Jaxson tells him, then

163

adds to Marie, "Fresh herbs to cook with, made by you? That's something to me."

With a pleased face, she waves him away as Justin and Jason come out of the house with Jason shouting, "Dad, tell Mom to stop cooking and come join us. Shit!"

Grams, who'd been quietly watching the children until this, shouts, "LANGUAGE!"

Jason calls over to her, "Sorry."

Justin tells Dad, "She's doing what she does," referring to our mother, not his.

"Being a perfectionist. I know. I'll get her." He slaps Jaxson's bicep as he passes. "Did you do that thing I told you about?"

"No, dad. I told you that *you* had to do it. Remember?" They share a stubborn look that says neither will budge.

As soon as Dad's out of earshot, I ask, "What thing?"

"Nothing. Dad's being Dad. Forget it."

"C'mere Jaxson!" Grams calls out from her comfy, cushioned seat. "Give me a hug, dammit!"

Jason laughs, "Hey!"

"I get to swear! At my age I've earned it!" Jaxson strolls over with a big smile for her, and pulls her into an embrace. "I've earned it!" she says over his shoulder to anyone listening.

Dressed less Hip Hop than usual since it's a family affair (plus our Grams always gives him a hard time for wearing his hats backward), Jason shakes his head as he says, "Beautiful hypocrite, that's you, Grams." He moves a couple dishes around to make room for a huge pot of the best chili on the planet, let alone Georgia.

Standing next to him, Justin snatches up a square of corn bread, takes a bite and loudly announces, "FUCK, that's good."

"Not funny, Justin. That's the last F-word I'll be hearing today," Grams grumbles, taking her seat. "Jaxson, talk Don out of sending our Jake away."

"God!" Our Uncle groans. "He'll be back!"

"I'm a big boy, Grams. Jaxson doesn't have to rescue me. I need to get away from all of you anyway."

She cocks a slender, silver eyebrow at me as her southern drawl sweetens the sour utterance, "Never heard such a stupid thing in all my life."

She's the only one among us with an accent since everyone else here was raised in the city. You can sometimes hear one sneak out of Dad and his sister, Marie, but it's rare.

When we sit down to eat, easy conversation flows throughout the meal. As the people I love most make me feel special, the guest of honor, I'm reminded of Drew's selfless act in giving me this time with my family, and all the attention that comes with it. My respect for her grows.

When Jax and Justin laugh loudly over Jason accidentally saying, "How'd we run out of Mom's homemade ginger-ale already? Fuck me!" and Grams slaps the side of his face so hard we all hear it, I grin with only one thought in my mind: *I wish Drew was here. She'd get a kick out of this.*

I stand up. "We're gonna be here a while, yeah?"

Everyone looks at me with silent questions.

Mom asks me with sarcasm, "You have someplace you need to be?"

Bracing myself, I explain, "I was gonna get my roommate and bring her over. She doesn't have any friends in town. She's alone, and I feel bad with us all having a good time. All this food."

Everyone is staring at me.

"Well, go get her!" Mom calls with a wave to hurry up. As I head out, my chest pounding, I hear them quietly filling each other in.

Mom asks my brothers, "Is he living with a girl-friend and didn't tell us?"

Uncle Don says, "No. Just a roommate. Nice girl. Just moved to town."

"Don gave her a job," Marie says.

"He *wants* her to be his girlfriend," Jason says.

"I heard that!" I call back, turning around and jamming a finger at him. "I just don't want to feel guilty when I come home and find her watching some dumb movie all by herself."

"He's bringing her here for me, Ma," Justin says, loudly.

"Fuck you, Justin!" I call back and head inside.

Grams yells, "LANGUAGE!!"

And everyone laughs.

19
DREW

Surprised, my head swings toward the sound of his key turning our lock. Jake strolls in wearing grey jeans and a light blue, short sleeved, form-fitting button-up, his hair perfect as usual. He frowns, locks eyes with me, and heads over to the couch, glancing to the flat screen. "What the fuck is this?"

"The Danish Girl."

"No no no no no. Get up. Put on that yellow sundress. You're coming with me."

Blinking at him, I slowly pick up the remote and turn off the movie. "The one I wore to the farmer's market?"

"Is that where you went?"

"Yes, the Saturday you were making a mushroom omelet."

His brain scans the memory, and he nods. "Yeah. That day. That dress. Go put it on."

"Where are we going?" I ask, thankful the dress is

washed and hanging in my closet. As I pass him, I breathe in how good he smells. Like charred coals and freshly cut grass.

"BBQ," he says, simply.

I freeze. "Your family's BBQ?" He nods with a look that says arguing is out of the question.

When I resurface from hurriedly putting on a little makeup, combing my hair, changing clothes and wracking my brain over how this happened, Jake appraises me and nods, "Beautiful."

My body lights up as his gaze drops to linger on my hips. A flush rises from my neck to my cheeks. He notices and his eyes narrow. "C'mon. They're holding dessert for us."

In his car, we are silent most of the ride. I can feel my heart beating in every part of my body, even my hair. I can't stand the question racing around my brain a second longer. "Why'd you change your mind?"

"About bringing you?"

"Yeah."

He shoots me a look before focusing on the road. "You're the one who said you didn't want to come, Drew."

"I didn't say I didn't want to. I said—" A wicked smile flashes from him. "Oh, you jerk."

He laughs then reaches over and lays his warm, wide palm on my thigh. "I didn't like the thought of you sitting at home by yourself when we were having fun. Didn't feel right." He releases my leg, and I stare at the spot where his hand was.

"That's very sweet."

"It's just decent, that's all," he mutters like it's no big deal.

Truth is, I *was* feeling lonely. I'd tried to study some of the self-help books I bought, but my mind kept wandering. Then I went to check out that movie, but a slow-moving period piece isn't a good idea when you're feeling like you don't have any friends.

"Thank you."

He glances over and holds my grateful look a hot second. There's a satisfied smile in his eyes as he turns back to the road.

"Am I going to meet all your brothers today?"

His lips go tight. "Jett and Dad don't get along. Jeremy, he's the youngest."

"I remember."

"Well, he just finished the thirteen weeks of training in Parris Island."

"That's right. He joined the Marines."

"Right. We saw him at family day right before you moved in, then he got deployed to Syria." Jake glances over to me with pride. "He's going to be a hero."

"He already is."

Jake nods. "You're gonna love Mom's chili."

*T*he house is immense and gorgeous, yet somehow homey. From the deep front yard and grand expanse of windows, I expected to find museum-like décor, but it's not that way at all once you're inside. It looks lived in. The furniture is welcoming you to sit down and take a load off. I guess with boys you wouldn't want a home you couldn't get rowdy in.

"Is this where you grew up?"

"It is. They're all in the backyard. This way."

He leads me through a kitchen that bears signs of a feast being made. It's fairly tidy though. Now I understand where Jake got his urge to clean up right after cooking. The smell alone causes my stomach to growl. Jake smirks at me.

"Guess I was hungrier than I thought," I whisper.

"Nah, that's my mom's cookin.' Your stomach

would make that sound here even if you'd had a seven course meal before you came over."

He opens the back door and the view hits me like a sunset you accidentally catch during a drive in the mountains. I fight the urge to go wide-eyed and awestruck, but it isn't easy.

Their yard is beautiful with trees as the frame, rather than a fence. Flowering bushes are tucked under a canopy of bright green tree-branches. There's a stone dolphin fountain to the right. The perfectly mowed lawn has several walking paths cut through it. It slopes down the further you go in. In the forefront, on the flattest surface of grass, is a long table where everyone sits, talking easily amongst themselves under strings of golden lights held up by four copper poles. Some people are laughing, others deep in serious debate. Off to the left sits a half-devoured buffet, the dishes covered in pretty, netted tents to keep the bugs away.

As Jake and I arrive on the back porch, everyone looks over at us. The discussions are abandoned as they rise to meet me.

I am beyond terrified.

I don't know if Jake can tell, but he takes my elbow in a comforting way and leads me down the steps to the grass, where they are heading to meet us halfway. I lean on his support and force a smile.

The thing about escaping a marriage like mine, that ended with such pain and lasted for much too long, is your confidence doesn't bounce back like a brand new rubber band. The elastic of my psyche is looser than I'd like, insecurities whispering to me on a day like today when I so hope to make a good impression on such kind southern faces.

Justin and Jason greet me like we're old friends, and I catch a wink Justin throws my watchful roomie.

Don introduces me to his wife, Marie, and I instantly see the resemblance between her and the man behind her who's sizing me up from a polite mental distance.

"I hope my husband isn't too hard to work for," Marie says with a smile.

"I've just started there. I'll call you if I have any trouble."

She laughs, and my eyes dart back to the man. Immediately I know he is Jake's father because he looks like the twins and the elegant lady standing next to him has to be Jake's mother. She has his darker details.

A nice woman introduces herself to me. "I work for the congressman," she says with a nod behind her. Inwardly I stiffen as my eyes flit over.

"Oh!" I thought he'd looked familiar. Thank God Jake told me to wear this particular dress.

He approaches me with his hand out. His wife is with him, staring like she's trying to see my soul or something.

"Michael Cocker. Nice to meet you, Drew."

"Nice to meet you, too, sir. I never put that together, that you were...I guess if your name started with a 'J' I might have."

He laughs, "That's Nancy's doing. She likes 'J' names."

"It's not just me!" Mrs. Cocker objects, reaching out to shake my hand. She clasps it between both of hers and tells me in a confidential tone, "My sister Anna loves 'J' names, too. We both took all the best ones for our children."

"Is she here?"

"No, they're in Savannah." Nancy looks at Jake. "Oh, I didn't tell my sister! She's going to be so mad."

"I won't tell her if you won't," Jake says.

Justin laughs, "I'm calling her tomorrow."

"You better not!" Nancy Cocker admonishes him.

Jake's grandma calls over from the cushioned seat. "Come here, child."

Jason warns me, "Don't you dare swear in front of Grams, Drew!"

Appalled, I look at him on my way to meet her with Jake holding my elbow again. "Why would I do that?"

Everyone laughs and I realize I've stumbled onto an inside joke. They all sit down and politely resume their conversations, but I can feel eyes boring into me.

Keep your head high, Drew.

You are safe.

"This is our Matriarch," Jake tells me, introducing her with her full name, "May Cocker."

"See, Nancy got that from me. I named my children Marie and Michael, only I used *my* letter, because I'm egotistical." She winks at me, blue eyes twinkling with humor. Instantly, I like her. "I don't know about this living with a man you're not married to, though. You women today don't know how to look out for yourselves!"

On a soft smile, I tell her, "Jake's very scary. I lock my bedroom door at night."

He laughs.

She wags a finger at him, eyes dancing. "You hear that! She's watching you."

"She has nothing to worry about," he smiles.

It's hard not to snort.

"You get her something to eat, Jake."

"I will, Grams."

There are two children off running around the bushes at the far end. I point to them and ask, "Are those your older brother's?"

"No, they're...where is Jaxson?" Jake says, under his breath. He turns around and asks the group, "Did Jax leave?"

"I'm here!" a deep voice calls from inside the house. A dashingly handsome, rugged and tall man appears. I glance to Jake and see his brown eyes glitter as his oldest brother strolls down the back patio steps onto the grass. Jaxson Cocker is smiling at us in worn-until-they're-softer-than-pajamas blue jeans and a plaid shirt meant for a party less formal than this one. Yet somehow he walks like a king, as most cowboys do. "Just had to make a call." His eyes flash to the Congressman where I catch a silent exchange. He nods to his father as if to say, *the deed is done.*

Sun-kissed in both hair and skin, Jaxson's eyes are a darker shade of green than his twin brothers, and have a depth to them that feels wise. He has an old soul, and I relax in his presence as he shakes my hand, staring at me like I'm accepted without question. "Hi. I'm Jaxson, but a lot of people call me Jax."

"Drew. Nice to meet you." I glance to Jake and find him watching me with an expression I can't read.

Jax nods toward the pretty food tents. "Have you tried Mom's chili yet?"

"No, but I hear it's amazing."

My roomie says, "Understatement," with a shake of his gorgeous head. He leads me over to the long table, and hands me a plate, pride gleaming as he explains, "These are brown sugar, sweet potatoes with marshmallow topping. That's apple-smoked bacon in the green beans, and red onions to sweeten the taste. And this right here, this is what you'll never want to stop eating."

"Jake, you're exaggerating!" Nancy calls over, genuinely annoyed. "I can't meet those expectations!"

He tells me, "She's modest. Ignore her," loud enough for his mother to overhear. Just like his brown eyes get stormy when he's irritated, so do hers as she huffs. They share a look that he has won the battle, but she's not happy about it.

As we walk to the table, my plate piled high, Jason tells me over the many conversations, "Lookin' good. But you're missing out on the best part, Drew."

"What's the best part?" I ask Jake.

"He's pissed the fucking ginger ale is gone."

"JAKE!" May shouts.

"You know you love me, Grams." He pulls out a chair for me, and takes the seat beside mine, his chuckle low.

As I take a bite of chili and close my eyes with awe, Jake bursts out with satisfaction, "Right?! What'd I tell you?"

He did not exaggerate, not one bit. "It's amazing, Mrs. Cocker."

She smiles, but then glances to her husband. "If only Jett were here to enjoy some."

The Congressman's jaw tightens. He shoots her a look.

She holds it, unfazed.

Jake told me that Jett and his father can't be in the same state together. Seems sad when everyone is so nice like this, and get along so well.

As I enjoy my meal and do everything in my power to make sure the attention stays on Jake since he's leaving soon, I find myself watching the family patriarch and wondering if it pains him not having one of his sons in his life anymore.

How must Jett feel, missing out on BBQs such as this one?

JAKE

I unlock the front door and hold it open for Drew. We've talked away the past three hours, finding all kinds of things we have in common. We both camped as kids with our families. Not the rented cabin type of camping, but the sleeping under the stars in a sleeping-bag kind. We both saw a bear once, both nearly crapped ourselves. I told her my favorite band is The Doors, and she started humming "Crystal Ship." That is the song I love most of theirs, which I told her.

She nodded and said, "Me too."

And that's just scratching the surface of our long conversation.

It was really comfortable being with her at my childhood home. I was nervous for her at first, especially with how my parents were watching every move she made. I found out later that they'd asked the twins about her when they discovered we'd all gone to the Gardens, so they were already curious. Seeing her in the flesh increased that, and I can't blame them.

They know I don't bring girls home to my family. None of us do. Jason did once, but he's such a fuckin' softie for waif-like blondes. He hasn't done it since.

Outsiders earn their way in, and so far no woman has with me. I almost brought a girlfriend home back when I was in high school but then I found out she'd fucked one of the teachers while we were dating. Grew even more careful after that.

Dad's assistant and her family have been coming for a long time, years of working with him and all. Our nanny used to come to the BBQs but she passed away last year, unexpectedly. Hit us all hard. And of course there's our Aunt on my mom's side, her husband and our four cousins, all around the same age as us. They're usually there.

"Aunt Anna is going to be pissed when she finds out I'm leaving."

Drew slides out of her pretty sandals and leaves them on our shoe-mat. "Is that your mom's sister?"

"Yeah. She forgot to call her. That's a sure sign she's upset. She hasn't said anything to me about going to Denver, either."

"With Jett and Jeremy gone, I'm sure she doesn't want to lose another son."

"Yeah," I mumble, slipping off my nice shoes and putting them next to my work boots. Shoving my hands deep into my pockets, I look at the beauty who sat beside me for hours and impressed every damn one of them.

Drew's watching me with a compassionate smile as she touches my arm.

"You have a great family, Jake."

"They're pretty good."

She nods and then looks at the door as a knock sounds. "Are the twins coming over or something?"

They'd better not be. I've got a plan to seduce Drew tonight and I don't need distractions. It's Sunday. I leave the day after tomorrow. I don't want to go without feeling her body under mine again. And again.

I want to imprint myself on her mind so that she doesn't forget me when I go away.

"Let's not open the door," I murmur, barring her way.

She whispers, "Seriously?" so whoever's on the other side can't hear.

I nod once and take her by the shoulders, looking into her gentle eyes. I'm about to kiss her when another knock interrupts, followed by a woman's voice, calling, "Drew?"

"Bernie?" she frowns, moving past me to open it.

There on my welcome mat stands a woman I never expected to see tonight, and hopefully never again.

Bernie Lancaster, ex-model turned high-class hooker, is dressed to the nines except for a couple tell-tale details: her hair is a mess and her nose is red from the blow.

As I realize they're friends, it slams into my head that there's no way Drew knows she hooks. She wouldn't be hanging out with her if she did. They're too different. Bernie is the best liar I've ever met. Fucking addicts. Lying is their gold-medal skill.

With pupils twitching, Bernie glances from Drew to me, and her fake smile vanishes.

"Why the fuck is *Jake Cocker* here?"

Surprised, Drew looks at me. "You know each other?"

"Small town," I shrug. "How ya doin' Bernie?"

"Not good, Jake," she snarls. "I've been better, and now I see your fucking face. Why is he at your house, Drew? You guys aren't dating. Please tell me you're not dating Jake Cocker." Her face is filled with so much disgust I want to punch her.

She's disgusted with *me*? That's a reversed table I never expected turned.

"This is his place, Bern," Drew quietly says, looking from the manipulator to me. "I'm his roommate."

"Oh!" Bernie exhales, but then her eyes narrow on me and her voice reverts back to disgust. "Oh," she repeats, this time flatly.

Don't have to ask why. I know *exactly* why she hates me. I cross my arms. "Can we help you?"

She dogs me with another death-stare. "Drew is like my best friend since forever, Jake. So don't look at me like I'm a piece of trash that rolled up on your door. Show a woman some respect, you fuck."

Drew closes her eyes with embarrassment, and says a low, "Ummm..."

Bernie cuts her off. "I'm being stalked, Drew. Can I come in??"

Waving her friend inside with a hurried, "Of course!" Drew starts for her room, pausing to reassure me, "We'll just go in there, Jake."

"Take off your stilettos first," I grumble.

Drew spins around, blue eyes flashing. "Okay, I don't know what your history is, but you are being rude and it's very unattractive."

"I don't give a shit."

"I don't deserve that shit from you, Jake," Bernie shouts, throwing her finger at me. "Especially you!" Her hand is shaking.

Especially me? The nerve of this chick.

I clamp my mouth shut, knowing there's no way this argument will end well. The two of them disappear, but not before Drew stares at me with all kinds of questions in her eyes.

Bernie didn't take off her shoes. Bitch.

An hour later, Drew's bedroom door opens. I'm on the couch watching "The Walking Dead" on Netflix, Season Two. Seen 'em all but only a show this good can distract me from what is goin' on in my house.

Drew appears, worried and much more distant than before. "Jake?" She glances to the T.V. and mutters, "Oh...Shane. I never trusted him," then looks back at me. "I think Judith is his. So sad."

181

"Doesn't matter now. Rick will raise her as his own."

"Yeah."

I lean back. "So?"

"Bernie's goin' to stay the night, here on the couch. And before you say anythin', please just let me say she's gotten herself into trouble. Not with the stalker." She's wringing her hands in front of her sundress. "I'm not sure there even is one, but she needs me. I'm not going to go into her personal details because that isn't polite, but do you trust me?"

Exhaling loudly through my nose, I nod that I do.

It's Bernie I don't trust.

Just then I hear footsteps padding toward us. The bitch took off her shoes after all. I've no doubt she did it to manipulate Drew, probably while crying about how awful her life is. As if she had no part in that. God, I'd hoped I would never see her again. After all we went through.

She rounds the corner, eyes much softer than when she arrived. I was right, her mascara's gone. Hair is smoothed down now. I can just picture Drew petting her and telling her, *it's gonna be alright. Let me help. I can fix everythin'* while handing her a million tissues.

"Fine. She can stay on the couch. But not tomorrow because it's my last night here and I need to get a lot done."

Glancing to Bernie, Drew says, "I'll stay at Bernie's tomorrow night. Okay, Bern?"

For a second I almost take it back because that

means Drew'll be gone on my last night. But having her bat-shit-crazy bitch of a friend here wouldn't do me any good. I keep my mouth shut and watch the two of them come to an agreement.

Bernie is looking at me like she's a child who's been damaged. She looks vulnerable and lost. I have to admit it's persuasive. I'm only human. "Thank you, Jake. I know I don't deserve the help."

I'm coming off as the asshole here, so I say, "It's not that. It's just...never mind. Water under the bridge." I stand up and head for my room.

Two women against one guy.

No man ever won this war.

It's why we fight against other men. At least *there* we have a chance at victory.

I just can't believe these two are so-called best friends.

This isn't going the way I had planned. I'd had it in my mind all night to get closer to Drew, take her again, sleep all night in her arms and spend as much time with her as I can before I take off. Naked, if I had my way.

That's shot.

She's gone tomorrow night?

Then I leave town.

This is bullshit.

I won't see her for who knows how fucking long.

My veins feel strangled, and there's nothing I can do to get that intruder out of here.

Bernie Fucking Lancaster is sleeping in my apartment. If you'd told me that would ever happen I'd have laughed in your face. Won't be surprised if she steals something. Nothing she does will ever surprise me.

"I'm going to bed."

"Do you have an extra blanket?" Drew asks.

"Yeah," I sigh, "Hang on."

Bringing it to her, along with an extra pillow, I receive a smile from Drew that makes me even madder. I want to kiss her so bad.

"Night, Jake."

"Night." I glance to Bernie, who offers me a shy, grateful nod.

Damn, she's good.

22

DREW

"Here, you can wear my pajama shorts," I tell Bernie as I rummage through my dresser. "And this t-shirt is really comfy to sleep in. Oh wait, you're tinier than I am."

"I don't mind," she whispers. "Baggier is better for sleep. Can't rest if you're in tight clothes."

"True. It feels like sleepin' in a python's belly."

She smiles and makes a face. "Gross."

"There's a draw-string on the shorts. Should be okay."

"I'm sure it'll be good."

For the moment it feels like when we were kids, just being together, comfortable. When I stayed at her apartment after moving to Atlanta I hardly ever saw this calm side of her. The cocaine habit has its claws too deep. She has guys over every night of the week, partying with them. Because I certainly wouldn't do the drugs with her. She invited me to, but I declined and she didn't push it, calling me a prude more than once.

People defend their bad behavior so they can keep doing it, my Pastor father taught me that. He's counseled troubled souls so many times, he learned that they'd be more inclined to work their tails off to make you seem like the wrong one than take responsibility for their actions...and change.

I'd always imagined Bernadette as this New York City to Milan to London, goddess. I drank in the pictures she shared on social media over the years since she'd left Dublin, and envied all the places she'd been, the fabulously glamorous friends she had, and the money that seemed to seep from her pores.

It was drastically different from my modest, small-town life.

But my naïve adoration and envy of her abruptly ended when I saw up close what that kind of exposure can do to a girl who doesn't have family roots to fall back on. Bernie's dad had always been absent and her mom wasn't the nicest woman I'd ever met. She pushed Bern to be a winner in pageants. Loved to show off her blonde, beautiful daughter wherever she went like she was a thing and not a person. "Look at this preciousness right here! Have you ever seen such a perfect child? She's gonna be a big star one day! You watch!"

"What happened with you and Jake, Bernie?" It's the second time I've asked her. Of course I wanted to pry as soon as I'd first gotten her alone.

"You know those Cocker boys. They're notorious. I don't want to talk about it, Drew. Okay?"

"Of course." Worried about what her answer might be, I ask her anyway, "Did he hurt you?" The anger between them was so fierce, I'm convinced they slept together. It's everything I can do not to demand she tell me. But I've never seen her so distraught as she was when I shut my bedroom door. Her story came out disjointed and hysterical until she was weeping.

Truth is, I almost don't want to know. Especially since I'd prefer to keep it secret how I feel about him. And how Edward is no longer the only man I've been with. The old Bernie I would have told, but this one...

She gives me a reproachful look for asking, walks to my bed, laying down the night clothes I gave her before she starts to strip. "I said I didn't want to talk about it."

"Sorry." Crossing to my dresser, I pull out something for me to sleep in. "Just want to make sure he didn't."

"Oh, he hurt me alright," she mutters with such anger that I cut a quick glance over in surprise.

Now I'm sorry I asked.

Dammit, they dated!

It's so obvious, but I didn't want to admit it.

And here I was thinking I was too old for Jake. Bernie's a year older than I am. She started school late.

As she yanks down her leather pants, my eyes widen. "Bernie! What happened to your behind?"

She looks over and flatly says, "He got a little carried away with the spankings."

"Who did?!!"

She shrugs, "Just a guy, Drew. Doesn't matter."

Flabbergasted, I toss my clothes on the bed, too. I can't stop staring at the purple marks. They are obscenely dark, ominous. As she pulls on my shorts and tightens the string as tight as it'll go since she's so skinny, she won't look me in the eye.

"That wasn't *carried away*, Bernie. That's abuse. Those bruises are deep, honey."

"They go deeper than that," she mutters, meaning emotionally and not just from this time. She's talking about way, way back to childhood. I know all about that. Her mother had a string of boyfriends. Some of them were okay, but some changed Bernadette's life forever. Pedophiles often prey on single mothers to get to their children. And her mom was too desperate for attention to notice.

My knowing about the abuse she suffered as a little girl is what gave me so much patience when I stayed in her apartment and saw how she was running herself, her life, and her future into the ground with white powder she never had enough of.

My offers to help get her off the drugs were turned away as though they were insults. She laughed in my face. The partying never stopped. I was forced to turn my focus solely to the reason I came to Atlanta. She preferred quick sand and slapped my hand away over and over every time I tried to drag her out.

So I moved in here.

Maybe she *wants* help now.

I will do whatever it takes to get her on her feet again, if she'll go to a rehab and get professional help. Addiction is way over my head, that I have learned.

Bernie slips into my shirt, her tiny, model-sized breasts disappearing from view.

I pull her to me and give her a big hug. "I'm gonna help you. There are lots of rehabs you can go to."

Her arms were loosely around me at first but as the tears really start comin' she grabs on tightly and buries her face into my shoulder, sobbing. Her whole body is shaking. I hold on and don't let go until her pain subsides. It breaks my heart into a million pieces. This isn't what I wanted for my friend. I would have loved to keep her on that pedestal, a model not just in magazine but of inspiration. But we're all just human beings doing our best. And some of us have deeper scars, like she said.

While I change clothes, she sits on my bed and wipes her face with a makeup-remover pad, the mascara long gone. Skin-toned smears cover the sheets as she keeps tugging them down her skin, staring off, numb.

We're silent, like sisters who don't need to talk to fill in the spaces. I pull a pillow off my bed and offer it to her.

"I don't think Jake's pillow is as fluffy as this one. His are flat guy-pillows he's had for too long."

She glances to me like a wounded deer. "You guys aren't dating, are you?"

Oh shit. Her face! She still loves him. The feeling

isn't mutual, that's for sure, but what am I supposed to say?

Struggling, I blink to my hands. "No, we're not. I have to be honest with you, Bern. I do like him. Oh my gosh, that hurts to say it." I give her a nervous smile, but she stares back at me, oddly.

"You know their dad's a congressman."

"What does that have to do with anything?"

"You can't trust politicians, Drew. They're liars."

"He seemed like a nice man."

Her eyebrows shoot up. "You've met Michael Cocker?"

"Yeah," I shrug, defensively. "I'm Jake's roommate. It's no big deal. He invited me over for a BBQ tonight since he's leavin' town for...a while." I feel protective of him suddenly, and leave out his moving to Denver.

Annoyance flashes across her face, making it ugly. Or maybe it's more than that, maybe anger and down-right jealousy. She turned away from me so quickly I can't be sure. As she stares at the wall, she asks through gritted teeth, voice forced more casual than she's acting. "You went to their house?"

"Yeah."

"Was it a big party like with other people, or just the family?"

"Why are you asking me that?"

"Just answer the question, Drew."

"Besides some people who work for the Congress-man, it was just the family."

She looks at the floor. "Huh."

Oh, now I get it.

She's never been there and when they'd dated, it gnawed at her ego. Especially someone like her who gets invited everywhere all over the world.

"It wasn't a big deal," I whisper, feeling guilty.

Her beautiful eyes cut to me, then something changes in her expression and she smiles. I'm thrown by the shift, but she explains it away with, "I'm tired. I'm goin' to bed. Or to the couch, or whatever. Thank you for the good pillow, Drew." I nod and she hugs me really tightly one last time, then kisses my confused cheek before she quietly whispers, "And for the shoulder."

In my doorframe, she looks back and gives me a sad smile. I see nine-year-old, towheaded Bernadette Lancaster standing just inside the front door of her Momma's home, waving to me with her cheeks flushed from the daily race we ran, trying to beat each other to the old Dogwood.

"Love you, Drew Charleybomb."

Feeling empty, I return her sad smile with one just like it. "Love you, too, Bernie Casteroil."

She closes the door.

I slowly sit on the edge of my bed, frowning at the past.

The world didn't give us what it promised.

23

DREW

I swear because of technology being so ingrained in our every day use, the vibration of my phone when a text comes through is hardwired into my brain. It's all the way in the closet, stuffed deep in my purse and still I can hear it while I'm dreaming. It's crazy.

I run to answer it, my head foggy from sleep, hair all over the place, and find the message is from Jake.

You were supposed to be here fifteen minutes ago.

"Oh my God!!!" I cry out, heart-rate zooming from zero to sixty. "I forgot to set my alarm!" Scrambling through hangers I chose an appropriate dress for work, plus shoes that match. My nude bra and panties get thrown on and I rush to the bathroom as I'm zipping up while throwing my shoes at the front door where they clatter like awkward dice.

Basic makeup gets applied with shaking fingers, and brushing my teeth is all I have time for. Lipstick will be applied at a stoplight.

"Where the hell did I leave my purse?!!"

Running back to my room, I grab it from the closet and dash out.

The door to Jake's room opens, which nearly makes me jump out of my skin.

Furious and relieved at the same time, I spin around to tell him that messing with me by sending fake texts is so not funny!

My heart stops.

"Mornin' Drew," Bernie says, rubbing her eyes. She's wearing Jake's shirt. The one he wore to the BBQ.

She yawns and stretches her slender arms high, giving me a full view of the fact that she's not wearing panties.

Can you punch a soul? Because someone just punched mine.

I careen backward, eyes tearing up. My lungs dry out. My heart has forgotten how to beat. I can no longer see straight.

With her hair disheveled, she leans against his doorframe and mutters to herself, "I really need some coffee. Slept all of twenty minutes last night. Well, actually, just since he's left. How long ago was that? Half hour? No, maybe forty-five minutes."

"Oh my God," I rasp over a lump of anguish. My eyes are stinging as I turn away.

He fucked her. All night long. And I'm the one who insisted she stay over!

I'm the dumbest woman who ever walked the earth. So naive. So gullible.

First Edward.

Now Jake.

I know she's beautiful, incredibly sexual, much more experienced than I am. I've seen her charm even our high school principal and he put Scrooge to shame! I'm sure the sex life they'd had before I came along was too hard for a twenty-five-year-old guy to resist once it was offered to him.

Was he that taken in by her? Or did she just climb into his bed, and he didn't turn her away? Did she knock, or was he grabbing a glass a water and saw her lying on the couch, looking like an angel as she probably smiled at him and crooked a finger.

I groan, heading for my shoes, "I have to go to work."

I have never felt so much pain.

At least with Edward, when he started cheating, I didn't love him anymore. He'd tugged me along for years never coming through with promises until I was too numb to think anything of him except a desire for his absence so I didn't feel so misused.

It didn't hurt like this. I'd begun to believe that Jake might care for me. That he brought me to that BBQ because of his feelings for me.

I didn't believe they were pity. The poor lonely

woman left home watching a movie really was the reason he came to get me? That was it?

"When do you get back, Charleybomb? You're still staying at my place tonight, right?"

Glass scrapes my veins hearing her call me that nickname right now, while wearing his shirt!

I slip on my shoes, dazed, and mutter, "I know I'm not staying here tonight."

"Oh honey, I thought you said you were just friends!" She pads over to me, pulling his shirt over her shaved self.

I croak, standing straighter, "We are. It's fine. I'll see you after five. I'll go straight there from work."

"You okay?"

"Totally."

I practically run outside, feeling vomit threatening. My Honda has never been driven this dangerously. At the office, Don is sitting at the front desk. His eyes leave the computer to meet mine as I enter the room. I'm all apologies. "I'm sorry. I didn't set my alarm."

He nods curtly, and with uncharacteristic coldness, says, "Don't let it happen again."

"I won't. I promise I won't."

Rising, he motions for me to take my seat. "I need you to go through these old proposals today, Drew. I've marked down the things you're looking for. We need to catalogue these in a way that help us write new proposals according to the successful ones of our past. This is the stack where we landed the job. This is the stack where we didn't. Find the commonalities. This is going to take weeks, so start slow. Small things. Make notes of verbiage, what we offered, the time frame in which we offered it. Start there. Reference this list, then branch out after you've completed it. Look for themes. Got it?"

I nod, reading the list to see if I have any questions. "I'll do a great job, sir."

He pauses and his eyes soften just a little. "Don't call me sir."

"Okay. Again, I'm so sorry for being late!"

He waves it away, but the softening vanishes as he tensely heads back to his large, private office. It kills me inside that I disappointed the man who's giving me this opportunity, who I sat across from at a BBQ last night, surrounded by his family! Does he think I'm taking advantage of the familiarity by slacking off? He must! And the worst part is, I don't see him again all day.

I wish I could say the same about Jake. As soon as he hears Don leave, he comes out of his office and heads right over to stand in front of my desk. My eyes dart up and catch the guilt in his eyes, and I instantly want to punch him in the neck.

"I should have woken you up. I had other things on my mind."

My eyes go tight. "Yes, well...it's my responsibility to wake myself. I'm a big girl. And I have to focus now. So if you don't mind."

He frowns and slides his hands into his pockets. "You're pissed. I can understand that."

"Why would I be pissed at you? You got me this

job." All I can see is him telling her what he's going to do to her next. "I'm indebted. I just want to do a good job, so I don't think it looks good if you are hanging out here at my desk when this huge binder needs to be read."

He walks away, footsteps lagging. I am intensely aware of each hesitant one sending him further away from me.

Good, go back into your office and stay there, Jake. Because I don't want you to see me cry.

I put all of my attention on doing my best at what Don needs of me. One agonizing hour later, Jake is finally sent away to the local job site, thank God.

Please don't come back.

I can't lose this job.

2 4

JAKE

*G*lancing to my phone, I see it's five-forty. I exhale and turn into the office's parking lot, intent on apologizing to Drew.

This whole day has been shit.

I should have done this before, just taken the ego down and said I'm sorry. Because I am. It was a petty thing for me to do, getting back at her since I was angry. But I acted like a child, and an asshole. I hope she forgives me.

When I walk in, her desk is empty. I look around for her purse, but it's gone. Heading back, I knock on his door. "Uncle Don? Drew take off?"

With his eyes glued to the computer screen, he nods. "Mmhmm."

"Shit," I mumble.

"I don't think I saw her smile all day."

"She was upset she was late."

Uncle Don spins his pen in his hand and regards

me with a wise look. "It was more than that. She made some good headway on that work I gave her, and I told her so. She just nodded and kept at it. Juan came in at one point and said hi to her and she barely looked at him. She looked shell-shocked, if you ask me. What happened last night?"

"I'll go home and talk to her," I mutter, turning around. "Talk to you later."

"See ya tomorrow...oh wait! Jake! Get over here." He follows me out and I turn to walk into a big bear hug. "You're flying out in the morning."

We slap each other's backs and separate. "Jason's driving me to the airport."

"Your family isn't going to be easy on me until you're back."

I chuckle, "Yeah. They really won't." Clapping a firm hand on his shoulder, I say, "And I won't apologize for that."

He laughs. Before I vanish through the door, he calls out, "She's a good woman, Jake."

I nod and wave without looking back.

When I get to the apartment, everything is quiet. I call into the void, "Drew?" with no response. After taking off my shoes, I walk to her room. The door is slightly open so I tap on it. "Drew? You in here?"

Nothing but silence.

"Shit. She's at Bernie's. How could I forget that?" The memory of Bernie knocking on my door in the nude, flashes before my eyes. I slide my phone out and text Drew.

An hour later, I text her again.

Hey, I want to see you before I go.

I wait for her response. Just when I think one's not coming, I get this:

I'm busy Jake. Have a great time in Denver.

I stare at it. "Fuck."

I dial her, but she doesn't pick up. Just her voicemail.

"Hey, Drew, uh, I'm sorry I didn't wake you. I was really thrown by the whole Bernie thing. I'm sure she told you. But I...don't know how long I'm gonna be gone for." Pausing, I confess, "I really wanted to see you before I left. Call me back. I'll come to you. Just text me Bernie's address."

I hang up expecting a quick response, but she never calls me back. She doesn't even fucking text me. The rest of the long night I wait for her. I do laundry, pack up, field calls from family, and stare at the fucking clock all the way until I lay down to sleep.

If she's gonna be that way, fine. I don't need this shit.

But as soon as I wake up, my fingers are on the phone and I'm texting her again.

I'm leaving.

Jason knocks at my door at eight-thirty, and I'm still staring at the phone. "You look like hell."

I mutter, "Yeah," grabbing my suitcase. He picks up the other one and waits while I lock the door.

"Drew already at work?"

"Who the fuck knows what Drew's doing or where she is or what she's thinking?" I head to his car, scowling.

With the sounds of rolling wheels bouncing off the apartment building's hallway walls, Jason asks, "Something happen between you guys?"

"Yeah, something you know a lot about."

"Huh?"

"Bernie Fucking Lancaster."

Jason stops walking. "What does she have to do with anything?"

"I'll tell you in the car. I have a plane to catch and you were supposed to be here at 8:20 a.m."

I can hear how pissed I sound, but I don't fucking care. My patience is gone.

25

DREW

*W*hat a nightmare.

I got absolutely no sleep at Bernie's and not because she was dancing her butt off with some sheik yet again. No men were there with us. It was just she and I fighting over rehab.

And I couldn't stop thinking about Jake.

I wanted to call him, but doing so would've been the dumbest, most doormat-y thing I've ever done. I've been a doormat too many times without knowing until it was too late. This one I have my eyes open and I can choose *not* to be. Still, old habits are harder to kill than cockroaches in the desert.

I longed to take Jake up on his offer to drive to her apartment and talk with me. Even with what he did—what they did—seeing him before he left was something I needed. For closure. I wanted to hear it from his lips why he thought it was okay to have sex with my friend. I couldn't just chalk it up to youth. It's more about character.

But even thinking of discussing it makes me feel small. What's the point in asking? Actions are louder than words. I have to respond to what he did, not the reason he'll give it, when it comes to something as gross as this.

But the night proved to be very full and distracting. Bernie didn't want to keep her promise to me.

"I really don't think I need a rehab, Drew."

"But you agreed to go to one!"

"I know I did, but that was before I had a good night's sleep at your place." Her smile makes me sick to my stomach. "And you were so good to me, it made me feel better. I think I can quit the coke now."

"I thought you said you didn't sleep last night. "

"Well, there are many ways to rest, Drew."

I gagged, but put away my own pain to explain to her, "Bernie, you can't quit something as addictive as coke without help. You need support."

"I've got you!"

I put my head in my hands at that, feeling absolutely spent of patience. "I can't be your savior. I don't have that kind of power. I tried!" I looked up, pleading with her to understand. "When I lived with you, I tried to help you. Hell, I even hid your coke one night!"

Her eyes flashed. "I *knew* that was you! Where did you put it?"

"I flushed it."

"You did *what*? Do you have any idea how much that costs, Drew?"

Defeated, I told her, "See? You wouldn't be so upset if you were really quitting now."

The anger vanished instantly. "I'm quitting! I am! I don't want this kind of life." Her eyes became liquid as she ran both hands through her flaxen hair. "I have to get out. You have to help me!"

"I want to. *Let* me help you."

"Okay!"

"Great. Let's go to the rehab." I grabbed my keys, but she snatched them from me and chucked them at her wall!

"I'm not going to fucking rehab! I'm not going!"

I was in over my head.

Again.

It went on like that for hours.

And now I'm sitting at work, feeling like I barely escaped an insane asylum, and so glad I have somewhere to be where I won't feel completely useless.

"Morning," Don smiles as he walks in.

"Good morning, Don. Were you at the site?"

"I was." He does a quick scan of the desk. "Making good headway, Drew."

Offering him a smile, I admit, "You're right. This will take weeks, but I don't mind. I like finding the clues. It's like a game."

He laughs in disbelief. "Most people would think this task is very boring!"

"Most people are tired of working in general. Not me. I'm just glad to be here." And boy do I mean that.

"My nephew's plane took off an hour ago."

Pausing, my smile falters. "I know."

Don studies my reaction. "Jason called me and asked for your number. Said not to tell Jake. Is Jason interested in dating you?"

I blink a few times, too tired to understand the question. "I don't think so. That would be really weird."

"That's what I thought. All of the Cockers are way too loyal to pull a stunt like that, when Jake clearly likes you."

He has a strange way of showing that, sleeping with my friend while I'm in the other room.

"I don't pretend to understand how men think, sir."

Don laughs outright. "That goes both ways with both sexes, doesn't it? I told Jason I'd ask you. Wouldn't want to overstep my bounds as your employer. Do you want me to give it to him?"

Why would Jason want to talk to me?

"Um...I don't think so."

"Alright then," Don nods thoughtfully. "I'll be in my office."

"Okay."

As soon as he's gone, I read Jake's text messages again.

I really need to stop doing this.

26

DREW

Turning my key in our lock, I slowly open the door and look at the mat just inside. The only shoes on it are my sneakers from the gym two days ago.

My chest slumps at the emptiness beside them, where his workbooks usually are, and I close the door.

It's so very quiet.

My eyelashes lower.

I stand still, listening to silence.

He's gone.

Really gone.

I live alone now.

Blinking in the darkness, I flip our light-switch on and glance toward the kitchen. It's always spotless, but now it looks vacant, abandoned. Sliding out of my heels I rub my sore big toe, gaze drifting to his bedroom door. The one where she walked out from, wearing his shirt, hair sexed up, yawning as if she hadn't ripped my heart out and laughed at it.

Why are there some people who are so good at closing off their feelings, and then there are people like me?

Walking to set my bag on his coffee table, I hesitate then tuck myself into the couch, stare at his flat screen for a long time with the power off, my dark reflection wishing I had never touched him.

Never crossed that line.

Kept my vow, my promise.

Then would I have cared if she'd spent the night in his room, his arms?

Hollowness spreads through my chest as I answer, *yes*, I would have cared. Jake and I have a spark of something special between us. I know it in my core, even if he stained it, permanently.

My trembling fingers slide over the grey cushion and I turn my head to follow their slow journey. He was here just the other night. Then *she* slept here... before she went inside his bedroom and changed everything.

Getting up, I walk to it, touch the knob and rest my forehead on his closed door. Shutting my eyes I whisper, "Don't go inside, Drew. It's not your room. This is not right."

The knob turns.

His king-size bed is made, navy blue sheets squared off under a dark-chocolate-brown comforter. There's one nightstand beside it, just one, as the bed is pushed against the wall.

No room for a girlfriend to get comfortable.

But one did.

Mine.

"Bernie, why him?"

As I stare at the bed, hot tears begin to burn my eyes. A lump edges its way uninvited into my throat as my forehead crinkles with resisted pain. I cover my face and will my feet to leave.

But they're walking to his closet.

Cologne bottles are pushed together on his dark walnut dresser. These must be the ones he uses least. I take off the cap of one and sniff it, nodding because it's not a familiar scent.

His is memorized.

"He's gone."

I live in his home.

Without him.

Why does it hurt like this?

"Jake," I moan, sliding to the ground and wrapping my head in my arms.

When we left the BBQ together, when he hugged everyone goodbye, I saw how much it killed him to move away from such wonderful people who loved him so much.

Maybe that's why he had sex with Bernie. He was lost, sad, doing anything to feel better.

Don't excuse his hurting you like this. If he cared

for you, truly cared, he'd never have touched her. History or no.

Maybe if he were still in love with her, and they were meant to be together...then sleeping with her would have made sense. But that feels so wrong it can't be right.

Wiping my wet cheeks, I leave his bedroom, shutting the door with a finality that comes from somewhere deep. Yes, I have feelings for him. But I come first, don't I? This vacancy doesn't have to mean I lose footing on what I came here to do.

My spine straightens as I walk to my own room. When I moved in here I knew that getting close to Jake Cocker could jeopardize my goals. Just because I succumbed to our intoxicating attraction doesn't mean I will throw those goals away. If I'm tired of being a doormat, then it's up to me to stop being one.

Am I strong?

I don't know.

I've never really tried to see.

As I shut my door, looking around the space I made my home, I'm curious if I can impress myself.

I sure am tired of letting myself down.

27

JAKE

Small apartment with no view and zip for light.

The hotel I slept in on my first night last night was a palace compared to this cave. But this is on Uncle Don's dime so I wouldn't pay that hefty per-night-rate another day. "You'll do month to month?"

The landlady, Mrs. Sheeren, rolls her eyes and nods as if she doesn't have a choice, since no one would want to live here for long. If a year lease could be locked in, she'd dance the jig in her housedress.

Nobody told her first impressions last. Or, from those sharp, jagged toenails, she doesn't care.

We go over the details and she ups the rent from when I'd called. Not in the mood, I grumble, "I'll pay the first number you gave me."

"Can't blame me for trying," she snaps.

I scan a small but clean kitchen, then a hallway that leads to the single bedroom I can see from here, with one closed door halfway between. "That the bathroom?"

She waves for me to take a look.

On my way, I open a few kitchen cupboards and drawers in search of small brown flecks in the corners—cockroach poop. That's where they'll be if a place is infested. But there's no sign of 'em. I nod approval, eyes dead as I walk the short distance to the bathroom.

My eyes land on an empty, plastic caddy in the shower, and the scent of Drew's freshly shampooed hair rushes into my consciousness. Suddenly I hear her singing, missing words, humming.

Closing my eyes, I take a deep breath. "No shower curtain?"

"You'll have to buy one."

I'll have to buy a lot of things. Smacking the wall, I walk out. "It's clean."

"Of course it's clean."

"I'll take it."

"You say you work for Likuss?"

"I'm running the Denver plant starting yesterday, yeah. Drove over on my lunch break so I could do this."

Her thinly penciled-in eyebrows rise. "You look pretty young for that big a job."

"I'm forty-eight."

She laughs a funny sound that makes me smile as she waves my lie away and pulls open her ragged, black bag for an application. Eyeing the sheet of paper, she stuffs it back in, making her shoulder dip. "If you're running a place like that, you've gotta be responsible.

This has been empty for too long." Pointing at me she warns, "Don't think I run a slum. This is a nice building. Of course it's clean!" Dropping her hand, she mutters, "It's just dark in this apartment. That's why it's so cheap."

Everything is dark in my life, I'll fit right in here. "It's perfect."

Pleased, she digs for the keys while I write her a check. She makes a joke about knowing where I live if it bounces, and we do the exchange, her explaining where the mailboxes are, me staring at keys I wish weren't mine.

I'm a big boy.

I'll make the best of this.

At the plant they had no clue I'm unhappy with the assignment. Every employee working there was relieved someone sober showed up to lead, and I will do exactly that. Especially since I found out Dwight has an anger problem when he's drunk. Two people quit last week. I'll get 'em back.

"You staying?"

"Huh?" I look up, drawn into the present. "Yeah, I'll stick around a sec. Have a good day, Mrs. Sheeren."

Another roll of the eyes, like a good day is for other people—those don't visit her world.

She has no clue that's her choice.

One thing our parents taught us is you don't whine or complain about shit unless you're willing to change it. You want to gripe while fixing a problem? Fine, gripe. But keep adjusting, growing, mending, breaking and rebuilding, whatever doesn't fit your idea of what you want for your own life. Dad always told us, *It might be hard to face a problem, but if you ignore them, they get louder until you listen. Don't wait until they're shouting.*

Pulling out my phone, I check for a message from Drew. Just my family has reached out, though. Nothing from the roomie I didn't get a chance to say goodbye to, or give her an explanation of why I did what I did.

"I'm not texting her again," I grumble, spreading my legs to stand in an empty living room as I scroll through furniture stores near me.

It takes me a second to notice I'm typing a text to Drew. Pausing, surprised, I swear under my breath, "Fuck it," and type away, reading it three times before I hit send.

I need to speak to you.

Shoving the phone in my pocket, I swear a few more times and lock up.

2 8

JETT COCKER

JUST OVER TWO WEEKS LATER.

ith the worn asphalt of Highway 25 blurred under my wheels, I nod to Honey Badger that the next exit will do just fine. Black eyes lock on me, long hair flowing behind him. His returned growl travels on the wind and disappears.

He's itching to get where we're goin'. True to his earned name, the guy is unstoppable and scary as shit to those he doesn't like, even if he is round and soft looking. Ya really can't judge a book by its cover without insulting reality.

Five Harleys veer right, cutting in front of a blue big rig who spots the patches on our backs—*The Ciphers,* in Old English font, and wisely decides not to honk. He doesn't want his cargo arriving late just because he had to go to a hospital. Not that we'd beat him up just for honking. But he doesn't know that. We *look* like a mean bunch, and we are, but only to evil fucks who need to stop picking on people who can't fight back.

Denver, Colorado.

Didn't think we'd be riding down this way again for a long time. Traveled the northern states for months, ever since spring began. It's well into summer now and I prefer coming to Colorado when it's covered in snow. I like to snowboard when I'm given the chance. The hills of this state are fuckin' incredible. It's a damn shame it's not winter. A damn shame.

Scratch makes fun of me for snowboarding, but only 'cause he can't do it. Won't even try. He rumbles on about me having a death wish.

We all could be accused of that, doing what we do. But when you fight for a cause as good as ours, you ignore all consequences, dire or otherwise.

"Ya got the address?" Fuse shouts over the wind, brown hair flapping.

I call out, "What do *you* think?"

He smirks, "Lead the way then."

"As if I was gonna let you lead it?" I shout back.

He laughs.

I know this terrain well. The street we're headin' to is familiar to me. Of our entire MC crew, my memory for directions surpasses all.

Fuse was just bustin' my balls about the address because that's what we do. It's the one similarity these guys and my brothers back home in Georgia, share. My brothers and I grew up giving as hard a time as we got, laughing whenever we didn't see it coming, and hearing from Grams that we needed to watch our mouths with her legendary, "Language!"

I miss Grams. Been too long since I've seen her. But with her comes him.

The rumble of five hogs announces our arrival and I see the piece of shit through the house window, peeking out it to see what the hell all this racket is.

"He sees us," Tonk mutters as we dismount, his long legs not nearly as experienced at getting off a bike as we are. Gangly goofball kid who wishes he were scary, in my opinion. The only reason he's intimidating is because of his size, and that's not good enough for me. But I didn't accept him into the club—that's not my job.

Ignoring him, I turn to the most dangerous one among us. "Honey Badger, you know what to do."

He growls, "Yep. I got the back."

Tonk looks at me. "What should I do, master?"

"Suck my cock until I glaze your beard."

"You wish."

Everyone laughs low and deep, blood pumping because it's go-time. Tonk heads for the side door. Honey Badger takes off running and, despite his rotund structure, leaps the fence like a prize-winning racehorse. Scratch, Fuse and I stroll up to be gentlemen and knock on the front door, with both of them looking behind us to see if we have witnesses.

We don't.

I've got my eye on the prize.

"What do you want?!!" comes a petrified voice from inside the house.

"At least he's not pretending he ain't home," Scratch says, impressed, thick southern drawl deeper than a hole that reaches China.

Fuse adds, under his breath, fists ready, "He's got balls."

I shout back, "Open the fuckin' door, Dwight."

Dwight Forrester shouts back in a shaky voice, "But what do you want?!"

"He's got a heat on," Scratch rumbles to me.

"No shit. Alright. Step back. I'm kickin' it in."

A loud bang sounds from inside. Then a scuffle. I suck on the inside of my teeth as I wait. The door opens and there is Honey Badger standing with a gleam in his ink-black eyes. One corner of his mouth tugs up to say, "Beat ya."

We walk in and discover Dwight groaning on the floor. I turn to Honey Badger. "Where's Tonk?"

"I didn't let him in yet."

Scratch and Fuse start laughin.'

"I'll get him," I smirk, walking past Dwight. I give him a kick to get his attention. "Hold tight, friend." I didn't kick him too hard, just enough. He needs to be afraid of us. The problem with addiction is the addicts won't change until they hit rock-bottom.

He reacts like the world is over. And for him, it kind of is. His whole life is about to change, for the better though it won't feel like that for a while.

"FUCK!" he groans, rolling into the fetal position on the floor.

The side door has a nice-sized window where I can see Tonk glowering at me. I tap on it and call through, "What? Ya didn't want to hurt your new manicure?"

"Just open the fucking door."

"You do it," I tell him, heading back to the living room. "Pick him up. Put him on the couch."

Honey Badger sneers at Dwight while Scratch and Fuse grab the guy and throw him onto a couch littered with one pizza box, loads of rank, used napkins and fast-food burger wrappers. There isn't an empty spot on the coffee table, either. It's covered with booze bottles—empty, all but one.

A loud crash in the kitchen later and Tonk grumbles into the room. He's our newest member. Also the youngest and the largest. He has a lot to learn. He knows this, which is why he's shooting bullets at me through his eye-sockets, but keeps his trap shut.

Dwight whines, "What do you want?"

"We want you to clean up," Scratch informs him.

Scared eyes dart around the garbage. "Okay! I'll clean all this up by today! But how did you know..."

"Not the mess, you lost fuckin' soul," I sneer, making it clear we are very serious. "You. *You* need to clean up. Get sober. This whole grief thing you've got goin' on? It's over. It's time to be a man now."

Dwight stares at me and croaks, "Who *are* you?"

"Doesn't really matter, does it?"

He shakes his head a lot. "How do you know about my son?"

"I know all about you. Friends of yours are worried. They need you. It's time to clean up and get back to livin'."

His eyes go red and he starts to cry.

"Oh fuck," Honey Badger groans. "Stop being a pussy."

"My son died! He was only twenty and his future was ripped from him! I taught him how to talk! How to do everything! And I'll never see him again! Do you know how that feels?"

The room goes quiet. Scratch has a boy, he's grown now but he's got one. So does Fuse, and Tyler is still a kid. The thought of losing him isn't anything he wants to picture, but that's what he's doing now.

We all want children of our own at some point. Being in the brotherhood has a way of cementing loyalty and family into your blood. Especially for me, since I come from a family so thick I'd take a bullet for any of them.

Nothing else matters as much as that.

But still.

"Listen here, Dwight. That sucks that your kid ain't here. It really fuckin' sucks. Nothin' is ever gonna make that right, but there is no way he'd want you livin' your days like this. You gave up drinkin' for him when he was a boy, right?"

"How did you know that?"

"Do you think he'd want his father eatin' fuckin'

crap like this and pollutin' his body with enough booze to drown a whale? You were running that plant. You inspired the men who worked under you. Who the fuck are you inspirin' now because I'm here to tell you that life ain't worth shit unless you're offerin' somethin' to it."

Dwight stares at me like he didn't expect profound truths out of a biker, but that's part of the fun of surprising people.

They underestimate our intelligence.

Always.

It amuses me.

Sometimes.

But not today.

Today I have a brother who's gotta go home.

Pulling focus, Scratch says, "Here's what you're gonna do." Dwight stares at him like a sponge thirsty for water. "You're going cold fuckin' turkey. We're not leavin' here until you're dry. You're goin' to AA meetings. We're takin' ya. Then, when you're good 'n ready, you're goin' back to work so that your son can look down and be proud of his fuckin' father. As long as it takes."

"I got goosebumps," mutters Fuse.

Honey Badger grumbles, "Shut up, Fuse."

I turn to Tonk. "Since you have an intimate knowledge of the kitchen, bring us the biggest garbage bags you can find."

He heads off without argument. I expected a sneer

at my dig, but he didn't do that. Didn't even frown. Weird.

We're standing vigil over a grey-skinned, shivering, clammy-ass Dwight after eight hours without a sip. He won't drink water. Keeps begging us for a bottle of harder stuff. It's ugly but it won't stay like this. It's darkest before dawn.

Scratch motions for me to step outside. In the cool night air, I follow as he heads to his Harley and opens up the leather saddlebag for his chew. Wadding up a quarter-size, he tucks it into his gums and cranes his head to check out the half-moon. "Ya see Tonk's reaction?"

I nod. "Don't know what it meant."

"His dad's a drinker. To this day."

"Didn't know."

"I did. Carter, the guy who brought Tonk to us, he told me all about it. Guy's a real fuckin' piece of shit."

"Seems to be the trend with us."

He narrows his eyes on me, turns his head and spits. "Except for you."

He's referring to my father, and I'm not in the mood. "Ya don't know what you're talkin' 'bout, Scratch."

Sizing up my tension, he shrugs. "I think I do. But you be as stubborn as you wanna."

"Whatever." I walk to my bike and climb on, rising

off the seat to slide keys from my back pocket. "You got this covered?"

"Yeah, we're on it. Weirdest job we ever had to do."

"Ain't that the truth," I mutter, bringing my baby to life. There's someone I've gotta see. He's about to get the surprise of his life.

29

JAKE

I can't fucking fall asleep.

This is driving me nuts.

I've been here sixteen days and have hated every second of it. When I'm not working, I'm bored. Got beers with some of the guys from the plant a couple times now, but then I have to come here and that's when my mind starts racing with thoughts about her. I hadn't realized how deep she sunk into my psyche until she was gone.

Jason said he was going to talk to her, but I told him not to do that.

Now I'm wishing I hadn't.

What am I gonna do, call him and confess that the woman's got me wrapped around her finger, all because she doesn't want anything to do with me?

Is it really that simple?

No.

I miss her smile. Her face turning pink as those

pretty blue eyes flick away from something I said to provoke her. I miss accidentally brushing her skin as we pass each other in the apartment. I miss waking up knowing she's in the other room. I think about those things more than I think about the amazing sex we had on my desk.

She's walking around the office with fucks like Hank leering at her. Uncle Don has been checking on my progress here and I asked if he was keeping a protective eye on Drew. He assured me he was.

Hank better not get any ideas.

Flipping over on my mattress, I groan in frustration and stare into the darkness.

I've texted her every single morning, sometimes just saying that I hope she has a good one. Every damn day. No response. Nothing. It's driving me bat-shit!

Who the hell is knocking on my door at this hour?

My feet drop to the cool floor and I trudge over in sweats and no shirt to look through the peephole. My eyes fly open. "Holy shit!"

"Yep! It's me, brother!"

Swinging open the door, Jett and I crash into each other, slapping each other's backs hard. Grinning, I let him in, checking out his patches as he strolls by me and looks around, cocking an eyebrow, grey-green eyes exactly like our father's narrowing before he says, "This is a dump."

I laugh and nod, glancing around. "The furniture is temporary because I'm hoping I don't have to live here long."

"Not happy?"

"Fuck no. But what the hell, Jett!? What are you doin' here? How'd you even know where I was?"

"Certainly not from you," he smirks, straddling the arm of my boring-ass couch.

"Don't pull that bullshit, Jett. I called you. You never return calls." Like someone else I know. *Stop thinking about her!* Rubbing the back of my head to clear it, I ask, "You want a beer?"

"Do birds shit in the air?"

I grab us two and pop the tops as I walk back to him, letting them rattle on the floor. I'll get them later.

"You really aren't doin' well, are ya?"

"What do you mean?" I look down at my naked chest. "I look gaunt or somethin'?"

"Nah. You just littered." Jett's arms go wide, comically announcing, "King Tidy just let two bottle caps sully the floor of his castle. I know you. Something is rotten in Denmark."

"Talkin' about castles, and quoting Shakespeare. Impressive from a Cipher."

My older brother laughs, "Fuck you," his big smile a welcome sight. His teeth are perfect, bright white, and his skin is tan from riding a Harley around the states. Golden skin makes his cropped, dirty-blonde hair appear lighter. He's almost too good looking to be a biker, but there's something dark glinting in his eyes that says he belongs there. I haven't seen him in well over a year. That's much too long, but I get it.

What he's doing makes him a hero in my book, no

matter what Dad says. But then again, I always looked up to Jaxson and Jett, the two eldest in that order, and the ones who paved the way for the rest of us, taught us things, made the mistakes before we did, showed us how to raise hell and get away with it. They caused so much chaos in high school that the rest of us had a reputation before we even arrived. I'll never forget the first roll call in freshman year chemistry when Mr. Bentridge paused and muttered, "Shit," audible to the whole classroom before he looked up and said, "Jake Cocker?" with dread in his eyes. I smiled and gave him a wave.

Taking a swig of beer I shrug, "Ah well, I'm not like you, Jett. I don't have the urge to roam like you do. I'm a homebody, so..."

"Not sittin' well with you, being away from our family, huh?"

"Nope."

"Well, I've got good news for ya. Might not be here much longer."

I cock my head, take another swig and eye with suspicion. "You look pretty sure of yourself. How do *you* know how long I'm stuck here for?"

His grey eyes flash with a secret he's having fun not telling me. He leans forward. "Maybe your replacement is comin' soon, I'm just sayin." He's locked on me as he smiles and takes a big swig.

I blink at him, wishing he was right. But he knows dick about Don's business. And he's so out of the loop on that front, my chest caves in with resignation as I grumble, "Ain't gonna happen, Jett. Uncle Don wants to give Dwight a second—no, a *fourth* chance—so I'm here until he gets his shit together and comes back."

Dirty-blonde eyebrows rise, smile vanishing as his eyes go dead. "You don't think that's happening soon?"

"Nope. I visited him a couple times. Guy's a mess. A drunk driver killed his son and now the guy's a drunk himself. Can't really blame him, I guess. But it's not lookin' good for me."

Jett's nodding like he finally understands. "I see."

I exhale, "Yeah," take a drink, looking at the floor. "Fucking sucks ass."

"Yeah, you'd think someone should do somethin' about somethin' like that," Jett grumbles.

"What can be done?"

He breathes in through his teeth, making a hissing sound as he weighs the problem. Rising up, he paces a bit.

"You want to take your jacket off?"

Jett looks over his shoulder. "Huh? Oh yeah. Sorry. Was in my head trying to think of how to help you." He peels off the leather and tosses it onto the couch, leaving behind a body bigger than when I saw it last. He used to box, always had muscles, but this is ridiculous.

"Shit, Jett, you're ripped."

"Same as you."

"You're bigger than I am."

"Comes with the territory."

"Still have the one tat though, huh? Aren't you

guys supposed to get one for the club?"

Jett looks at the matching tat all of us brothers got when we each hit eighteen. Jaxson and Jett thought it up, and Jeremy designed it even though he was the youngest. He's got a way with a pen.

Jax and Jett got inked at the same time, together, since Jaxson was twenty and Jett was already eighteen at the time. We joined as soon as we hit legal age when Dad couldn't argue. I think he secretly wished he could get one, too. And I know he's proud of how we feel about each other no matter how different we are. You can see it in his eyes.

Jett holds my look a second, our tattoos on his mind, the years of history between us hovering in the air as he explains, "The Ciphers want me to get one. I'm stalling. I have our code written above my cock, though." He runs a hand over the crotch of his weathered jeans. "I'll get the tat of our patch when I feel like it." He glances to his right pectoral muscle where the etched C is permanently fixed into his skin beneath that t-shirt.

I nod, proud and a little relieved that he's holding onto his blood brothers over his chosen ones still. Sometimes I wonder how much he thinks about us, now that he has this new life. That we're on his mind, it hits me deep. I love the guy more than I can ever tell him. Nice to know I'm not forgotten when he's out there saving the world.

Staring at him, I quietly say, "Sure. Makes sense."

We're silent for a moment.

"What to do about Dwight...what to do about Dwight. Hmmm."

"Jett, it's useless. Let's just drink some beers and you can tell me about the shit you've been doing."

He waves me away, pacing in those big motorcycle boots of his. Finally he stops. "Well, I wish Jaxson had called and told me to drive down from Montana where I was nailing this farm girl with big tits so I could come here and fix Dwight up good so *you* could come home. I wish he'd have called and asked me to do that." Jett looks at me, eyes glinting with meaning.

I nearly drop my beer. "Are you fucking kidding me!"

"Nah."

"That's why you're here?!"

He grins the smile of a man who's done bad things. "Oh, yes. Dwight is in a hell of his own making right now."

"What the fuck have you done?!" I'm laughing, but also a little worried about Uncle Don's friend.

He fills me in on The Ciphers' plan, and what they're going to do. I'm listening, mouth lax from concentration and hope, and when he gives me the approximate amount of time he thinks it'll take, I shake my head and hold up a hand for him to stop.

"First of all, what the fuck, Jett, thank you. You really think I can go home in a month?"

"If I'm good at scaring him sober, three weeks maybe." He sets down his empty bottle and slouches onto the couch. "We'll stick around while he starts up at the job again. That'll give him a reason to stay clean. And he'll have a purpose."

As I stare at the floor, stunned he and his club have done this for me, I say under my breath, "We all need one,"

Checking out his dirty boot, Jett mutters, "Fuck yeah, we do."

Thoughts of Drew fly into my mind. A month, maybe less, and I'll be face to face with her. She paid rent. I know she's still living there. If I can get her to talk to me, I'll make her see...

Distracted, I offer, "I'll get you another beer."

"I'm good."

I blink up to Jett, walk over to sit on the coffee table, set my bottle by his, and rub my head. "Jaxson did this?"

Jett's smirk fades and his eyes go dead. "It was Dad, Jake. Dad wanted you home."

All the air leaves the room. Jett's looking at me, because we both know why Dad would do this. He hates having any of us gone. He hates Jett for leaving, especially since it was for a life on the other side of the law. He hates that Jeremy left, too, but to join the Marines, so that's a whole different thing. It's honorable what Jeremy's done.

Tooling around the country in a motorcycle club doing God knows what, not so honorable.

My voice deepens on the heavy topic, "You spoke to Dad?"

Jett shakes his head once. "The bastard made

Jaxson call me. Which he did. He didn't want to, but he finally did it, because Dad wouldn't let up and wouldn't do it himself."

"How you feel about that?"

Jett shrugs. "I feel nothing."

That's a fucking lie right there.

I bite my tongue from calling it out since he's too raw on this subject. I can't imagine how bad it would feel to have Dad not wanting to talk to me. "Right. Sorry if him doing that for me brought up some shit for you."

"Forget it, Jake." Jett plays with a stainless steel wolf ring on his finger, blinking at it. "Truth? His asking me to step up for this, in the way he knew I would, makes me happy to do it. Even if the hypocrite knows my methods ain't orthodox, he's still asking me to do this mission. Kinda makes me feel like, *fuck you, Dad.* Guess even you need people like me, huh?" We stare at each other for a good long second before he rises to go. "Well, this has been warm and fuzzy and all that, but I have a detox to attend." He laughs and puts on his jacket, changing the painful subject. "You should see this guy. Fuckin' mess."

I nod, thinking about how Dwight got that way. It doesn't slip by me that Jett and Dad have a painful father-son love. I wonder if Jett doesn't feel this mission —as he called it—isn't uncannily in the vein of his own problem. A father who wants to connect with his son, but can't.

I won't ask. Jett's a profound thinker. I'm sure he

231

knows. And he changed the subject for a reason. Men don't pry. It's not how we operate. We respect the right to man-cave. Listen when someone wants to talk.

Ask once, then drop it.

"Hey, Jett, Ciphers don't care that this'll take a while?"

"Nah. They owe me. Scratch, especially." His boots clomp to the door.

I follow him. "Well, we've got a few weeks in the same town."

"Let's grab a beer night after tomorrow."

Grinning like only a younger brother who misses one of his heroes can, I say, "Cool. Great."

He clamps a hand on my shoulder and shakes it. "You look good. Any women in your life?"

"Uhhh...not really."

He cocks an eyebrow. "That's not a no."

"It's a conversation for when I see you next."

"Fair enough."

"Hey, did Jaxson call you during—"

"—The BBQ? Yeah. I told him he should have waited until after. It made me miss Mom's chili." He winks and heads out, but I saw distance in his eyes. It's not her food he misses.

I close the door, stand here staring at the crappy apartment, the bottle caps on the floor, the uncomfortable couch. The news that I'm going home soon simmers before I grab my phone, dialing.

"Hi, this is Drew's phone. Leave a message. Thank you."

Huffing, I wait for the fucking beep I've grown to despise. "Drew. It's Jake. I'm coming back to Atlanta in about three weeks. Wait for me." I hang up and dial another number.

"Hey Jake."

"Jaxson, you bastard, what did you do!"

He chuckles and asks, "Has the plan gone forward then?"

"Yes, it's gone fucking forward. What the hell?!"

Jaxson's deep base lowers. "It's all Dad, Jake." He pauses. "I think Dad wants to reach out to Jett, but he doesn't know how. This gave him an opportunity, in a weird way."

"Really weird. But he may have just...you know."

"Saved someone's life. I know."

"Yeah."

"And Jett's the one saving it. Maybe Dad can respect him after this. Maybe there's hope."

"Maybe." I walk over, turn the deadbolt and head for my bedroom. "Anyway, I guess I have to say thanks."

"What took you so long?"

"Fuck off."

Chuckling, we hang up and I scan the one shitty dresser that's still empty, the lame mattress on the floor, and my two open suitcases I've been living out of since I got here.

Too excited to sleep, I start to unpack, muttering to myself, "Might as well, now that I know it won't be forever."

J've listened to Jake's message twenty-two times. Walking up to our apartment after a productive work day, I finally delete it.

Then I press 'undelete,' and listen once more, standing beside the spiral staircase I've never climbed since I moved in on the first floor.

There's his deep voice again.

Determined.

"I'm coming back to Atlanta in about three weeks. *Wait for me.*"

I whisper, "Oh God," as the line goes dead. Every time I listen to those last three amazing words I remember the night he proclaimed that if he still felt the same way about me when he got back from Denver, he was going to make me his.

But it hasn't been that long yet.

Of course, he feels the same way.

And a man often wants what he can't have.

I delete the message and hit 'Clear all,' banishing it to wherever deleted, heart-breaking messages go. Is there a room somewhere where angels listen to them, saying things like, "Oh, how sad..."

I guess it's time to find a new home. I can't live with a person who did what he did, and now won't leave me alone. Is this how he says he's sorry? Pretending like he didn't fuck Bernie all night long while I slept past the start of my workday?

Why is life so damned hard?

I unlock the door, and scream my lungs out as I see a man standing inside!

"Drew! It's just me!" Jason shouts with his hands reaching to soothe me.

"Jesus H. Crimminy, Jason! What the hell!" I grab my heart and gasp my breath. "You scared the daylights outta me!"

"I'm sorry. I have a key. I should have left a note on the front door or something. Wasn't thinking." Laughing, he takes off his baseball hat, rakes a hand through his light-blonde hair and says, "You should have seen your face. Shit, that was funny."

"Not funny, Jason. *Not* funny," I mutter as I slip out of my flats and leave them on the mat. "You're wearing your shoes. Would you take them off please?"

"You sound like my brother."

"I'm just trying to be respectful."

He throws up his hands, "Yes, ma'am," muscles flexing under the sleeves of a loose t-shirt emblazoned with a photo of Prince. Leaving his sneakers behind, he follows me into the kitchen.

I need some water. I'm nervous, now that the initial terror has died down. Jason being here isn't entirely unexpected. Last week Don asked me one more time if he could give *this* nephew my number. Why Jason wants it is a mystery I don't care to solve.

"So, how's it been without Jake?" he asks.

I shrug, "You tell me," pretending to be polite and not curious as I add, "How's your family handling him being far away for the first time, what with Jett and Jeremy gone?"

Watching me, Jason jumps to sit on the counter, socks swinging. "Nice memory, Drew."

"Well, it's your family."

"Uh huh."

"Stop looking at me like that."

He smiles widely. "Like what?"

"Like you know things you don't." I motion for him to let me into that cupboard he's blocking. He bends and I reach past him, grabbing two glasses. With adrenaline pumping, I pour water and hand him one.

As he glugs down half the glass, I head away on a casual, "Okay, see you later."

He starts laughing.

I whip around. "What?!"

"I didn't come over here to watch Jake's T.V. I have three of my own."

"You have three T.V.s?"

"Yep."

Sighing in resignation, I jut my hip out and lean on the kitchen island. "Okay, then why are you here?"

He loses the smile, clears his throat and sets down the water. "I want to talk to you, Drew. It's not an easy subject. I guess that's why I haven't come earlier." He jumps down and walks toward me. He's much taller than I remember, and from the look on his face, whatever he's about to tell me, it isn't all light and roses. "Let's go to the living room."

"Is it that bad?"

"Well...yeah."

He motions for me to lead the way. What could he possibly have to tell me, a relative stranger, that is so dire? My heart is pounding in my ears as I tuck my legs underneath me on Jake's couch, and grab the throw blanket I bought so I'd have something of my own out here. It's faux fur, very comfy, and I wrap it close while waiting for him to sit, and rearrange his baseball hat a couple more times as he preps himself. He's staring at Creative Loafing on the coffee table. "I haven't got that issue yet."

"Jason!"

"Sorry. Right." He faces me and blurts, "It's about Bernie."

I bristle, tightening the blanket around my body. "I don't want to hear this, Jason. I don't want to hear you apologize for your brother. He's a big man. He can do it himself."

Ice-green eyes blink at me. "Why do I have to apologize for Jake?"

"Are you kidding me?!" I start to remove the blanket and leave, but he reaches out and stops me.

"Hold on! Hold on! Let me just say what I came all the way here to say. It's not polite to not give me the chance, is it?" He cocks his head with sincerity shining from his pale-green eyes.

Playing the have-some-manners card to a southern woman. How can you argue with that, Drew?

I sigh, "Well, that's not fair."

"If it's what I have to do, then I'll do it. For Jake."

I'm confused and reticent, but I was raised right and you don't turn someone away when they ask for your ear. Not where I come from. You hear them out and THEN you walk away.

"Fine. Go ahead. But I'm not happy about this."

"I know." He sighs and does that thing with his hat again.

I pull my knees up and tuck the blanket back around me. "I'm waitin'."

In a fit of frustration, Jason throws the hat across the room. It flies and hits Jake's plant. "I was in love with her."

My jaw drops. "With Bernie?" He nods. "You and Bernie?"

"I thought she was the most beautiful woman I'd ever seen. And I'm in the music business." He shakes his head to imply that he's seen some beautiful women, but they didn't compare to her. Rubbing the bridge of his nose he explains, "She was a model. So we both ran in the same fucked-up circles." His eyes lock with mine. "Drew, she was in love with me, too. At least, I think she was. I'm not really positive on that, because the drugs fuck with her and who knows what the hell she feels anymore." He shakes his head as memories clog his mind. Lost in the past, he looks away from me.

I am utterly stunned.

Jason and Bernie.

Jake slept with his brother's ex?

That's even worse than what he did to me.

Honor is honor. If you don't have a moral code to stand by, you fall. And you take down the people who love you.

Jason groans, "Ah Drew, it was a hard time. I got into drugs when I was with Bernie. You don't understand. I thought she was everything. I'd never met anyone so damned easy on the eyes, and she's real good at making a man feel special. But when I met her she was already using. She brought me into it. The two of us together, it was a fucking disaster. Our bank accounts got sucked dry. Work vanished. Justin told Jake and Jeremy, and they both called Jaxson and before you know it, I was in the middle of a fucking Cocker Brothers intervention."

Frowning at how painful that must have been for all of them, I whisper, "I'm so sorry, Jason."

He lays his head in his hands. "It's okay. I wasn't addicted to the stuff. Not really. I don't have that gene. But I *was* addicted to Bernie. Even when I went cold turkey under their orders, I ignored them when they said to leave her. I stayed with her, followed her around like a bodyguard. I begged her to let me take her to rehab. She wouldn't go." He looks at me with real pain in his eyes. I nod with compassion, silently telling how much I understand that part of what he went through. "Things got worse, with all the...guys..." Jason rubs his face with both hands and shakes his head out like a dog after a jump in the lake.

I whisper, "She has a lot of admirers," remembering all the men who were always at her place. "She's very beautiful. Even in her addiction."

He nods and looks at me with an expression like he wants to say more, but the story's too big for just us. "Yeah, a lot of admirers," he says, almost to himself.

"Why are you tellin' me this, Jason?"

"Because I want you to know that when she knocked on Jake's door..." He pauses. The idea is just as hideous to him as it is to me. "...it was to get back at me. She hated that I fell out of love with her, that I stopped coming around after months of her refusing to get help. And maybe—God I hate to say this, but I know her, so it's probably true—maybe she did it to break your feelings for him, so *you'd* stay with her."

So he's okay with Jake having sex with his ex-girlfriend? He forgives Jake? And why didn't Bernie tell me about Jason? My brain is spinning as I whisper, "I don't have feelings for Jake."

"Because, Drew, she's very manipulative. It's the drugs. It's not her, but the drugs *are* her, now." He rubs his face again, moaning, "God, I fucking hate cocaine. I'll never touch the stuff again." Jason's shoulders start shaking and I realize he's crying, that he's been holding it back, and lost the fight. I was too consumed by the story to see. Reaching over, I hug him. He leans into me and rasps, "I loved her so much," covering his face.

"She's lovable. She really is. I'm sorry, Jason. I'm so, so sorry, but you can't blame yourself. I know that sounds cliché, but clichés exist because they're very common truths." I pet his head and whisper, "Bernie won't quit until she wants to quit."

He nods and sniffs, pulling away in a manly, I-can-handle-it fashion. Wiping his eyes, he won't look at me anymore. "Yeah. I know. It sucks."

I sigh, "It does," handing him a corner of the blanket.

Without hesitation he uses it to dry his cheeks. "Don't tell my brothers about this, okay?"

"Never will. I promise."

Staring forward on the couch next to me, with his nose all red, we sit silently for a few moments before he retrieves his hat, smoothing down his hair before putting it on. "I've got a busy day in the morning, so..."

"Yeah. Okay." I get up to walk him out, but he stops me from following.

"No, stay. I know the way." A charming smile flashes as he meets my eyes to share a secret. "My brother likes you."

"Oh? Well, I hope we can be friends."

That hurts even to say.

Holding my look, Jason shakes his head once. "He likes you more than that, Drew. And P.S., I don't remember him ever bringing a girl to a family dinner." Bowing dramatically, he corrects himself, "*Woman.* Excuse me. Not a girl." He spins around with style and heads off.

I wait for the click of the front door before I'm able to breathe again and I don't move for a very long time. There are so many thoughts swirling now that he's told me his side.

They were in love, he and Bernie. Or at least he was in love with her. She might have loved him. He's right, who really knows what Bernie feels anymore? I doubt even she has a clue.

Oh Jake...why'd you have to sleep with her? Was she really that hard to resist? I saw you melt when she thanked you for letting her stay the night. I saw the look on your face, the same one I've seen on so many men's faces when she casts her spell.

Why'd you break my heart like this?

31

JAKE

"I told you not to talk to her, Jason."

His voice is as clear as if he weren't over a thousand miles away and out of punching range.

"Sorry, man. Had to."

"When was this?"

"Well, you're coming back tomorrow so it was, what..." He pauses. "I don't know. More than two weeks back."

And she still hasn't called or texted?

That's not good.

"He fucking talked to Drew behind my back," I mutter to Jett who's sitting beside me at Lincoln's Road House.

Through a calloused, cupped hand, Jett calls out, "You're an asshole, Jason!"

He laughs. "Tell him I said it takes one to know one."

"I'll do that," I mutter, my mind on Drew. Jason

hasn't seen Jett since over a year ago, so he wishes he could be having a beer with us right now. "I'd put you on speaker but the music is too loud."

"I can hear that. The Eagles. Predictable."

"Jason hates the Eagles, apparently," I mutter to Jett.

Jett shouts at the phone, "That's because Jason likes that Hip Hop bullshit."

On an amused chuckle, Jason confesses, "Fuck I miss that guy. You're so lucky."

"I am. We've been hanging out a lot. It's been good." I look over at Jett who stares ahead with a smile in his eyes. Not one for sentimentality, he won't admit aloud that he feels the same as I do.

I think he needed to reconnect with me as badly as I did with him. Or maybe he just needs his family back in his life.

Back to the subject of Drew, I say, "Well, I hate to tell you this Jason, but it didn't work. She hasn't responded to my texts."

"What the fuck? Well, that's weird, man, I don't understand it."

I mutter, "Women."

We hang up and I lay my phone on the bar, staring at the thing that's been tormenting me ever since I left Atlanta. Can't stop checking it for any sign of her. If it rings, my heart punches my chest, then deflates. I think I liked it better when we just had land lines and you could escape the noose for a few hours at least.

Gwen, the bartender whose ass Jett has been

tapping for the last week or so, smiles at him as she strolls up. "Another round?"

"Oh yeah," he smirks.

"Sick fuck."

"You know it, Gwen."

She grins over her shoulder as she sashays away. But he turns toward me, and doesn't watch her exit. I doubt they'll hook up even one more time, knowing my brother. He didn't watch her walk away, and his flirting feels mechanical.

"Dwight missed a meeting today."

I stare at him, stomach turning as I realize what that could mean. "You're shittin' me."

"I am not."

"Did he fall off the wagon?"

"Not yet. But I think we went soft on him. Tonk's connected with him more than the rest of us, which Scratch saw comin'. But I told Tonk he's gotta stay tough. It's not a man we're fightin'. It's the disease." Jett glances over as Gwen pops tops off our bottles and sets the frosty fuckers down. "Thanks, babe." He hands me mine and we tap them together. "Thank God we don't have that bite, man."

"Pure luck."

"Ain't that the truth. Because I would hate to stop the days when I enjoyed a cold brew." He takes a good-sized gulp and sets it down on the counter, hard.

"Hey!" shouts a guy shaped like a bear. "Your name Jett?"

I glance over first since the guy is in my eye-line.

Jett turns around really slowly to take a look. "Yeah?"

With fire shooting out of his ears, the guy barrels up. "You're messing with my brother!"

"I'm not into men, Grizzly Adams. No matter how hairy."

"You callin' me a—"

"—I'm tellin' you I'm not interested in whatever it is you're sellin'." He motions up and down the hulking frame. "No matter how ugly."

The guy's arm reaches back to punch Jett. Jett ducks in time then punches the guy in the stomach.

It's on.

I leap up as two more guys jump off their chairs. Some men just love a fight.

I'm one. Especially with all this pent-up frustration I'm dealing with.

One comes at me and I use his velocity to shove him nose-first into the bar counter. He grunts as blood gushes out from the crack in his bridge. His buddy punches me in the gut as reciprocation. I elbow him in the chin, sending his teeth chattering and his jaw offline. Not giving up that easily, he tries to grab me. I dip out of reach and punch him in his ribs three times.

Jett's using agile, trained punches the guy can't get ahead of, not for lack of trying. My brother is a trained boxer, went semi-pro before The Ciphers. He throws his opponent, and the guy crashes into a table and takes it down with him.

Jett turns to me and sends a front kick to the

broken-nose fucker who was coming at my back without my knowledge. The guy makes another pain-filled grunt as the wind vanishes from his lungs.

An uppercut later and the one I'm fighting has to go to the hospital for his jaw. He probably should have quit after I jammed it the first time. Now he's going to be drinking out of a straw. Maybe he likes smoothies. Who knows?

I took a couple hits, but nothing lasting.

Gwen calls over with a smile, "Cops are comin,' boys!"

Jett shakes his head and walks to the crumpled mess on the floor. "I'm guessin' your brother is Dwight?"

Bloodied and delirious, the guy barely nods.

"We're helpin' him, you dumb shit. Stay out of our way and you might still *have* a brother." Jett shakes his head in disgust and looks at me, walking away. "Let's go."

I throw some cash down for Gwen, finish off my beer, and stroll out after my big brother.

Just like old times.

I've been jumping in my skin.

His plane arrives today, but I don't know when. Nothing I do can help me concentrate on these proposals. I've completed the initial cataloging of what worked and what didn't work for the company. And now it's my job to see if I can find any nuances I missed that might help them in future negotiations. I'd been doing a great job at it, quite frankly.

Until today.

Every time the office door opens and I hear male voices, I freeze and forget to breathe. I'm not a fan of Hank, but the others are nice. Some are quiet and keep to themselves. Juan is in here the most so he and I have had some nice conversations since I first started working here.

But if he talked to me today, I wouldn't remember any of it.

I hear the doors open just after lunch break, where

I opted to stay and work. Don walks up to my desk and hands me a take-out bag. "Got you a burger."

"Thank you. You didn't have to do that."

"Ya gotta eat."

If I can keep it down.

"You're very sweet." He walks by and Juan comes crashing through the doors with Matt chasing him.

"Give me that!"

Juan laughs, "Make me," running by my desk. They race around and Matt finally pins Juan, who's much smaller in size, and takes back the crumpled bag.

I ask, smiling in confusion, "What's in it?"

Juan yells, "Porn!"

Matt mutters, "Asshole," glancing to me and then quickly away. Apparently it *is* porn.

They head outside to the trucks so they can return to the site now that break is over. My phone vibrates and I lift it up, knowing it's him.

Can you come over tonight?

Frowning, I didn't expect to hear from Bernie, and I realize Jake hasn't texted this morning. I guess he's not going to, now that it's after one o'clock. This is the first day he's missed.

Oh Bernie, I just spent a difficult afternoon with you three days ago. What do you want from me?

And yet, there is always the hope that today will be the day she's ready to clean up. I want to be there when she needs a ride to rehab...and the support of a good friend who only wants her happy.

I start to type, but a deep voice interrupts me.

"Hi Drew."

My thumbs freeze on the keyboard. I look up and lock eyes with Jake Cocker, handsomer than I remember, and dressed in jeans and a black t-shirt that makes his eyelashes look darker. His determined and irritated stare bores into my soul.

"Jake," I croak.

Drew honey, this is gonna be harder than you thought! Stay strong. You can do this.

His voice lowers so as not to alert Don he's here. "Why haven't you returned my calls? Or texts?"

I blink twice and set the phone down, gathering my scattered wits. "Straight to the point, I guess."

"Yep."

"Because I didn't *want* to."

"Look at me."

I whisper, "No, Jake."

"Drew. Fucking look at me."

My eyelashes flutter up.

He crosses his arms, muscles tightening the cotton across his pecs and broad shoulders. The man was *meant* to be naked, only the last person to see him so was her!

"What?" I demand, temper flashing. "I don't have to respond. Welcome back by the way. You don't have to worry about this awkwardness we have between us now. I've been looking at places and I think I found something I can afford on my own."

Anger darkens his features. I inhale sharply and try to look away, but I can't!

"You're moving out."

"I think it's best."

He glares at me, snarls, "Fuck," and marches to his office where he slams the door.

I whisper, "Oh my God," touching my heart as it pounds with fresh pain. Shaking my head I croak, "Dammit!"

For the rest of the day he acts like I'm not here. He laughs with the guys when they greet him, "Good to see you, you fucker!"

He and his uncle chortle away in the big, private office about things I can't make out. Is this how it's going to be? Or will he settle down and act a little kinder?

The clock moves at an agonizingly slow pace. I keep checking it, hoping for the best, tortured when it shows only ten minutes have passed, then five, then two. Don't look at it anymore, Drew! Just don't look! When it finally ticks to freedom, I am out of here so fast my hair flies up from the wind of my racing heels.

"Drew!" he shouts.

Oh, you're going to acknowledge my existence now that I'm out of your clutches?

"Leave me alone," I tell him, nerves shot after being ignored for five straight hours. Rummaging for my keys, I race to my car, the clumsiest I've ever been as gravel crunches under my feet.

Why won't the damn key get in the damn lock?!

He runs over, literally sprints to catch me before I

escape. Just as I get my door open, he slams it shut and barks, "Enough. This is enough."

"Enough of your fake laughter, you mean? Enough of you walkin' by me over and over and pretendin' I don't exist, ignorin' me like I'm a piece of lint or somethin'?"

His jaw clenches, glare furious. "You didn't want to talk to me, so I didn't talk to you."

"And this is why I can't date someone in their twenties!"

"Because you won't even *talk* to them, or answer a fuckin' text? Kinda hard to date when you won't even open your mouth, Drew."

"I meant, because you're immature!"

"What's mature about what you're doing? Pretty sure you don't know what that word even means."

I blink through fury. "Screw you!"

He plants his arms on either side of my old Honda, jailing me in. His handsome face, the one I've missed more than I want to admit, is very close to mine. The heat of his breath is panting on me, and tiny flecks of gold pulse in his brown eyes as he struggles to understand, "Why won't you talk to me? I don't get it. Just because she made a move on me? I can't help what women are going to do. Especially when it comes to my family."

"Not because she made a move, Jake! Because you fucked her! Apparently for hours!" He blinks at me, stunned that I'm calling it out so boldly. I let him have it, everything I've been holding onto since that morning and all the mornings since he broke my heart. "Because I woke up to find her wearing the shirt you wore to the BBQ! The one you took me to because you were pretending to be a nice guy! Imagine my surprise when I find her panty-less, coming out of your room and sayin' how much sex you guys had, when you didn't even want her stayin' over! Did you have to say yes to her? I know she's more beautiful than I am, but she's my friend, and you said all those great things to me, Jake. Why'd you have to take her into your bed after you said those things to me? Why?!"

He shakes his head, helpless.

Spent, defeated, I whisper, "That's what I thought. Now, please release me and let me drive home. This day has made me very tired."

He surprises the hell out of me by kissing me out of the blue! Shocked beyond anything, I try to push him away, but he wraps his arms around me and pulls me against his hard body. "I thought you just didn't care about me, Drew," he rasps against my lips.

"What the hell, Jake?! You can't kiss me like that after what you did!"

In the middle of the fucking parking lot where we both work, Jake laughs and kisses me again, crushing my body and doing everything he can to melt my resolve.

Shoving at him, I croak, "Stop it! You're not bein' nice!"

He grabs my chin, forces me to look at him. "I didn't fuck Bernie, Drew. I tossed her back on the couch and locked my door! She lied to you. She lies! I wouldn't touch that woman with Juan's dick! Jesus, what kind of an asshole do you think I am?"

I whisper, stunned, "A big one?"

"Didn't Jason explain how I know her, why I can't stand her? She almost ruined my brother! If we didn't knock him into his senses, he would be fucking homeless by now!"

"I... I guess he didn't make it clear that..." I'm blinking hard, mentally replaying my talk with Jason. "I was wondering why he didn't mind that you slept with his ex."

Jake grins, "What a fuckin' mess. Now stop fighting me because I need to kiss you. *You taste like home, Drew.* Come here." He crushes me to him, our mouths melting together.

This time I give in as my brain pushes the last puzzle piece I thought I'd lost, into place.

Bernie lied!

She must have snuck into his bedroom after he left for work, stripped, and put on his shirt. When he told me he was distracted—why he didn't wake me before he left so that I wouldn't be late for my new job—that was probably because she had tried making a move again, or simply he just wanted to leave because she flat out disgusted him.

He must have been mad at me for inviting the person who hurt his brother, into his home and telling him he was being rude! Oh my gosh, I had no idea what I'd asked of him that night.

With all the *missing him* I've been feeling, I kiss Jake Cocker back as hard as he's kissing me. I welcome his tongue claiming mine, dancing as our kiss grows deeper, my heart overflowing with happiness.

Like he can't wait to touch bare skin, his hands drag down my back as my soft fingers eagerly slip into his hair. The kisses are so emotional, both of us desperate for each other.

If it weren't for the applause, he probably would have taken me right here in public against my car.

We break apart. I'm panting as our co-workers shout and holler, all of them back from the site now that the workday is over. Jakes grins down at me and I stare up at him with an awestruck smile.

On a chuckle, Don asks the men, "Who's next for Jake's welcome home kiss?"

"Oh! Me!" The guys all yell, raising their hands.

Jake laughs, "Idiots." He opens my car door and lets me in. "I'll see you at home?" I nod, glance over to the guys, and blush like crazy.

Juan waves to me with just his fingers.

Ridiculous. All of them.

I call out, "Bye, weirdos!" as Jake goes to close my door.

"Bye, Drew!" they sing, teasing me with fluttering eyelashes.

I cannot get home fast enough.

DREW

I watch him take off his work boots, eyes flashing to me. I'd been waiting by the door, nearly bouncing for joy with anticipation of his arrival. I might have broken speed limits on the way home.

Backing into our living room, I blurt, "I can't do this if we're going to be casual."

Tugging off his shirt and tossing it onto the floor, he smiles, "Mmmhmm."

"I mean it, Jake. Stop undressing."

"You really want me to stop? You don't want to see me naked?" Flexing his gorgeous chest, he undoes his belt. "You don't want my cock, Drew? You sure about that?" He drops his pants, steps out of them, pulls off his socks, and palms his erection. Holy oh my goodness. I forgot how beautiful that tip is when it's full like that. "You don't want me to fuck you...harder than we did in my office?"

"Stop. I mean it. I *want* that. You know I do, but I am not looking for temporary. I want the whole package."

"You mean this whole package?" he asks, stroking himself and walking over to stand in front of the flat screen TV. He's better than any show on television.

I yank my attention back up to his face. "Stop it! You know what I mean."

As his cock grows, he groans, "Marriage...babies... that whole package?"

"Yes. God, Jake, that is distractin'! But yes! I want those things. I mean, I don't need them tomorrow. We hardly know each other. And maybe I won't want them at all! I mean, we might be horrible travelers."

"What do you mean?" A smile tugs at his mouth.

"On road trips, we might be terrible together. That would be bad."

He rasps, "Awful. It would be a disaster," eyelids heavy, cock throbbing in his moving hand.

I'm pulsing in my panties, knowing how good it was to have him inside me before. The time apart has only increased how much I ache for his touch.

But I'm dead serious about what I want from a man who I am sure to fall in love with, if I'm not already there.

Lord help me, who am I kidding? I am deeply gone when it comes to Jake Cocker.

Steeling myself, I inform him, "I won't settle for being your fuck buddy. It could never work for me."

"No? Not even with this?" He holds his length out in his palm. "It's a good vintage. A very good year. Have a sip."

"This isn't funny!"

"It's a little funny, Drew." He walks up. "Now get on your knees and wrap your lips around my dick, because I haven't fucked anyone since you, and I'm crawling out of my skin to be in that sweet pussy again."

He pulls me to him with one hand and slips his other under the hem of my dress, finding out how damp I am. I moan, breathless and aching, "Jake, I can't!"

"Shhhh. Open your eyes, Beautiful. Let me get a couple of things straight. I am falling in love with you, and that's a first. I couldn't think of anything but getting back to you the whole time I was in Denver. I *ached* for you. More than I missed my family, I needed to hear *your* voice. I don't know if it's the way you blush, or the sweetness in your eyes, or the way you wanted to help your friend when she showed up here high as a fucking kite, or how great you are pretty much everywhere you go. People like you. I like you. Even my family likes you. My Uncle said you're impressing the shit out of him."

"He did?"

Jake chuckles, "Yeah. But who cares about him? You're impressing *me*. And now...oh God, you're so wet." He slips a finger inside and closes his eyes at the pleasure it gives him to feel for himself how much he turns me on. "Now I'm going to fuck *my girlfriend* if you don't mind."

My pulse pounds at the new title, lighting me up with happiness, shock, and a little bit of fear. To trust a man again—I don't know if I can do it. But I have to try.

Unable to look at him anymore, dizzy from what he just confessed, I dip my head to kiss my way down his chest, "I'm too old for you."

"Bullshit," he groans as my fingers wrap around his cock and start to stroke. Instantly, his hips move with me. I fall to my knees, look at his engorged tip and give it a lick. He growls, "That feels so good!"

Inspired by the dirty talk we did before, I whisper, "Cum in my mouth," before taking him in, heart pounding at being so brazen.

Jake fists my hair, but lets me control how deep I go. He's so big I need to use my hand to help.

He growls, "Say it again."

I moan, "Cum all over my lips, Jake," licking him from base to tip and cupping his balls gently with a warm hand.

"Oh fuck, you're killin' me. You know how much I fantasized about this? Get up here." He pulls me up, and rips my dress to get it off of me, throws the broken thing aside and steps back to look at me. "You're beautiful, Drew. I know you said your friend was. But bullshit. She's got nothing on you. Fuck, baby. I have jacked off to fantasies about your hot little cunt maybe a thousand times since we met."

Hoping it's true, I whisper, "Jake, you mean that?"

He nods, eyes primal. "Take off your bra."

I unsnap it and free my breasts, the pink tips tight little stones.

"Touch them."

Sliding my hands up my stomach, I take my time before I cup the soft underbellies then lift my breasts for him to watch.

"Bring them up to my mouth."

Rising to my tiptoes, I offer him my sensitive nipples for his pleasure, and mine. He pulls me close, one arm wrapped around my lower back to arch it, the other pushing my hand out of the way so he can touch me. I give myself over to him as he nibbles, licks, suckles me like he's got all the time in the world and nowhere else he'd rather be.

Sensing I'm growing light-headed, he instinctively lifts me, cradling me in his strong arms as his free hand massages my pussy. "I love it when you moan in my mouth like that. I'm going to fuck you like the greedy slut you are."

I cry out, appalled, "Jake!" but I can't deny how hot that sounded. Still, I won't go down without a fight. "Don't call me that!"

"My greedy slut, that's you, baby," he grins. "Greedy just for me and only me, huh?" He walks us to the couch and puts me over the arm of it, my ass in the air. Sliding my panties down my excited legs, he stares at my ass for such a long time I turn bright red. Everything is burning for his touch. "Say what you are."

"I will not say I'm a greedy little slut, Jake Cocker!"

He swats my ass, not too hard. "You just did." A thick finger slips inside me and I release a moan, closing my eyes as tingles spread.

I'm clutching the cushion as I hoarsely whisper, "Okay, I'm a greedy little slut, but only for you."

Chuckling with need in his voice, "Yeah, you are," he starts finger fucking me from behind, Dropping to his knees, Jake pushes his tongue into my pussy cave, grabbing my ass with both hands and pulling my cheeks open. I cry out as, at the same time, his index finger flicks my clit in tiny whispers. I'm so wet, so open. All I want is his gorgeous cock.

An experienced lover, he knows how sensitive a woman's body is when she's this aroused, so his finger dances around my fickle little bean with intuitive skill, sometimes lightly, others a little more quick and hard. I am grasping the couch cushions, moaning, inhibition gone as I crane my ass like a cat's.

His groan vibrates my swollen folds as he commands me, "Tell me what you want."

As his second finger slides inside, oh-so-slowly fucking me, I am such a mess I cry out, "Your enormous cock!" and shove my face in the couch, whimpering, "But those are good, too."

He laughs.

Turning my head I add, "I want you to fuck me until you send me to the hospital."

He laughs again.

"Until I never think of another man again."

The laughter stops.

He lays on my back, molding his body to mine over the couch's arm. His erection is pushing against my asscheeks, and I know how good this is about to feel.

He grabs a good fistful of my hair and growls right in my ear, "Done."

So fast that I gasp with intense pleasure, his cock fills my swollen, aching pussy from behind. Jake groans with all the relief of wanting me the entire time he was gone. He bites my shoulder and goes to work, pounds me so hard with the desire to imprint himself on not just my body, but my soul.

There is only Jake Cocker.

My disastrous roomie.

The torture I moved in with.

Is now mine.

"Don't ever mention other men to me again, Drew."

Smiling to myself, I whisper, "Other men," and he does what I want...starts fucking me harder.

He snarls, "You want to play like that, huh?" pulling my hair and clawing into my hip.

Every rough thrust fills me to my core.

As the orgasm builds to where it won't turn back, I moan, writhing, "Other men!"

"Fuckin' stop it," he growls, then roars, struggling against his own climax. "Oh God!" he shouts, slamming our bodies together. He's so hard and I'm so wet. This is what I was made for.

I start to tremble, completely lose it as he says, "I'm going to fill you with my cum so deep I'll be dripping out of you for weeks."

"Promises, promises," I moan.

"Fuck!" he shouts as his cock grows harder. "Say it. Fucking say you're mine."

"There are no other men, Jake. Your cock is everything I want. Just you, Jake. Just you, baby."

He roars again, fingers digging into my hips and my ass as his cock quickly strokes me. I'm throbbing now. The tight little burn of oncoming pulses are all I feel as Jake pulls me up and kisses me while we fuck like this.

Our tongues lash.

Bodies tighten, clench.

Waves of heat pulse from his into mine.

We gasp together as his juices explode, making my cunt contract and pound with each burst of fresh penetration.

Roughly kissing me, Jake's muscular arms grip me to him as he releases everything he has to give me. It's delicious and raw and complete. As the shockwaves ebb and I go boneless, he lifts and lays me down on the couch so he can climb on top of me and collapse.

"Sweaty," he murmurs into my neck. "We're fucking sweaty. I love it."

I whisper, "You're incredible," kissing his earlobe.

He rises, looks in my eyes, and says, "I just want something casual. I hope that's okay."

I squeal and hit him really hard. He busts up laughing. "I'm kidding!"

"Jerk."

"Yep," he murmurs, burrowing into me. Within seconds I hear snoring. Amazing.

*M*y phone, true to form, wakes me with a muffled text all the way across the room in my purse. While we slept, we must have changed positions because Jake's spooning me with his back against the cushions. I slip out without waking him and his arm falls off the side of the couch, hanging limp.

So jealous of how deeply men can sleep.

Oh, shoot. I forgot Bernie texted me earlier. This is her again, asking if I'm coming.

It's important. I need you.

I told her not to text unless it was serious next time. I even threatened to stop being her friend if she lied again. Knowing now what she did, how she lied to me about having sex with Jake, I'm fighting with sticking with that promise.

Because as I stare at these words—*it's important, I need you*—all that's going through my mind is, maybe she's ready for rehab! Oh, God, I hope so. And I can't risk not being there the one time her hand is really outstretched, hoping for freedom from addiction.

I can't turn my back on the chance.

Glancing to Jake, I consider waking him. He won't want me to go.

Coming, Bernie. But I can't stay long.

I slip my phone in my purse and tiptoe naked to my room to put on some clothes. Maybe I'll be back before he even knows I'm gone. Slim chance, but, that's okay.

Sometimes it's easier to say sorry than to ask permission.

♨

*B*uzzing the security intercom in Bernie's building, I check my phone to see if he's texted. Can't ignore him anymore. I don't want to scare him, or piss him off.

Well, maybe I could piss him off a little. His reaction to my taunting him with the words "other men" sure was fun.

"Hello?" Bernie's scratchy voice comes through the speakers.

"It's me, Bern. I'm outside."

"Oh, Drew!" She sounds a little too happy. I know what that means. "I'm so glad you could make it. Come on up."

The door unlocks with a loud honking buzz. Something in me hesitates. Why did she say she was glad I could make it like she's a polite hostess? My gut is telling me I'm not going to like what I'm about to find.

So I buzz her again. She answers, "Hello?" this time with confusion.

"Bernie, I was thinking you might be calling me for...well, to help."

"I am! Drew, what are you waiting for?" she asks with unusual jubilation. "Get on up here!"

The security door honks again, lock giving way for my entrance. Now I'm curious. What is up with her?

I enter the building and look over my shoulder as the door closes with finality. The foyer is quiet, my sneakers soft on the tile floor.

She opens her door after my first light knock with a flourish, as though I'm her favorite guest, the one she's held the party up for. "Finally! So good to see you!" She takes in my jeans and blouse. "Guess you could have worn something nicer, but still, come in! Guys, this is Drew! My best friend in the whole world!"

She ushers me in before I can ask her, *what the hell is going on?* Two large, ugly men in suits, turn at my confused entrance.

They take me in like I'm dinner.

"She couldn't wear a dress?" one grumbles, motioning to my body.

"This isn't what we paid for."

Paid for?

Bernie takes me by the arm and explains with a large smile and overboard enthusiasm, "Drew's an All-

American type. She's like a virgin type, sweet and all that. You'll love her."

I yank my arm back. "Bernie, what the hell?"

Her eyes are tweaking, pupils large, nose red-tipped, nostrils dotted with white powder around the edges.

And she looks terrified.

That smile is an act.

Oh shit.

Bernie's a hooker.

How did I not realize?

My heart races as I stammer, "Umm...I have to go."

"You're not leaving," one of the men says.

I smile as flirtatiously as I can and correct him, "Change! I have to go change! I thought the party was at ten. Bernie said she'd loan me her black Valentino. Right Bern?"

"Yes!" she painfully grins then says to the brute, "She looks GORGEOUS in that dress. You'll love it."

The two men walk closer to us. The one with the big nose, lifts up my hair and smells it. Sickly goosebumps of terror race up that side.

"She smells like cologne."

Oh hell.

I smell like Jake.

Of course I do.

"Sorry, last customer. I'll just go freshen up."

He doesn't argue with this. Which makes sense, in a weird way. No man paying wants another man's smell on you, I would guess. Bernie tries to follow me, but they stop her.

"Ah ah ah. You're staying here."

"Well, where else would I want to be?" she coos.

I disappear into her room and scramble for my phone, texting Jake. I'm too scared that those guys would hear my voice if I called. I can't trust Bernie if I dialed 911, I know that. She might act like nothing is going on just to save herself from being arrested.

How did I not know *this* is what was happening all those nights she had so many men over? I just thought she was a little slutty, and I blamed it on the coke.

Oh my God! It hits me suddenly that Jason telling me, *"All those men,"* in that weird tone was him testing to see if I even knew she was a prostitute.

And I was living here when she was doing it!

I feel nauseous.

Jake. I'm in trouble. I'm at Bernie's. There are two bad men here.

My thumbs hover over the keys, and I decide not to mention they think I'm a hooker. Instead, I hurriedly type,

Please save me.

Copying it, I paste it into a new text, sending the same cry for help to him three times, that way hopefully he'll hear me and wake up. Then I dial him and set the phone down.

"Drew!? Hurry up!"

"Sorry, just a minute!" Shaking, I quietly lock her

bedroom door, and pace. I hate leaving her out there, but hopefully they'll wait until I get back before they do anything sexual.

Stalling is the best chance I have to save us both.

She was hoping I could. I know that now. It was in her eyes. That's why she needed me. Not to have sex with them, but to think of an escape. I bet one of them is who bruised her so badly. She's scared out of her mind.

My phone lights up.

I rush over and hang up to text:

I can't risk them hearing me call you.

Staring at the door, I wait for his reply.

I'm coming! Does she still live cross from Ansley Mall?

Relieved, I type back that she does as banging sounds and one of the men grunts through the wood, "We're waiting!!"

I force a smile and call back, "I'm glad you're so eager. Hold onto that, big boy!" wincing at my own cheesiness. How does a whore talk to her trick? I have no idea. I've only seen movies about stuff like this. Only this is real life, and I'm so scared I can barely see straight.

Running to Bernie's bathroom, I turn on the shower and shout, "Be just a few minutes!"

"Drew!" Bernie's voice is shaking. "Don't wash your hair or anything crazy."

No, we wouldn't want to do anything crazy, Bernie.

For fifteen minutes, I sit on the bed with the shower running and them yelling through the door. Bernie laughs it off over and over, and keeps offering them more vodka. When she asks them for more coke — "*I just need a little bump*" — I drop my head into my hands and start to cry, just like Jason did when he remembered how hard it was to let someone you love, go.

Harsh yelling on the other side of the door sits me upright. Bernie's attempts to placate them has come to an end. They're over it. I leap back on the bed as the door comes crashing in. The guy with the big nose kicked it down and now he's seeing me still dry and in the clothes I came in wearing.

"What the fuck!" He sees my phone. "She called the cops!" he bellows to the other beast. I scramble toward the headboard as he runs at me, leaping onto the bed to tackle me.

"I didn't call the cops! I promise!" I try to dodge him by rolling off the side, but he gets ahold of my shirt and the fabric pulls me to him.

Bernie runs in, screams, "STOP! DON'T TOUCH HER!"

The other guy punches her in the back of the head so hard that her eyes roll back. She grunts and falls to the ground, blonde hair floating as she drops.

I scream her name. Try to run to her.

Big nose hisses, "I'm getting what I came here for," pulling me onto the bed and yanking the button off my jeans.

I kick and bite at him, screaming, "STOP IT! GET OFF OF ME!" He's pinning me with one hand, unzipping his fly with the other. He's having trouble with his suit getting in the way, flapping around with my struggle.

"Fucking stay still, bitch!" He slaps my face really hard and grabs both my arms, holding them above me on the bed with one hand as I fight.

"GET OFF ME!!!"

A crash sounds in the other room. Two seconds later Jake leaps onto the bed, yanks the guy back by his lapel, and punches his face hard as he goes down. Big Nose rolls backwards off the bed with a loud grunt. Jake dives onto him and hammers his face with fists that won't stop.

Panting with adrenaline, I stand on the bed, look over and see Jason pummeling the other guy just outside the door. Or maybe that's Justin? Yes, it's Justin, because Jason is leaning over an unconscious Bernie, lifting her head and whispering to her.

"Jake, stop. Don't kill him!" Grabbing onto his shoulders, I try to pull him off. "You'll go to jail! Stop it! I'm alright! I'm okay!"

He's seeing red, but at this he turns his head to make sure it's really true. He stands up, and pulls me into his arms, rocking me, voice thick with emotion, "Oh my God, baby, did he hurt you?"

I croak, "He was about to. You got here just in time," before I break down, sobbing.

Jake looks over his shoulder and kicks the guy.

"Fucking animal. Hey Justin! Call the cops!" He kisses my head a few times, then pulls back to see my face, inspecting it.

I whisper with so much sadness, "I didn't know she was selling her body."

Jake nods on a deep frown. We look over to Jason as he tells all of us, "The back of her head is bleeding. Justin, tell them we need an ambulance, too. I'm going to keep her where she is, in case he fucked up her spine. Can't take any chances."

I pull away from Jake and go to kneel with him. "Oh, Bernie. What happened to you?"

Jason and I share a look that only people who've ever loved an addict can understand.

*A*t the hospital, I watch my brother closely to make sure he isn't falling under the witch's spell again. Justin and I exchange a look, thinking the same thing.

As they moved her from the ambulance gurney to a regular bed, she told him he saved her life, with those big doe eyes she uses when appealing to the opposite sex. I saw them after she played Drew like a fiddle that night. And I've seen it before, used on poor Jason, successful every fucking time.

My jaw clenches, but the doctor addressing Drew switches my focus. "Let's see that bruise."

My eyes narrow as I turn to discover her face, which I thought was just red from fear since she flushes easily, is now showing marks on it. "You said he didn't hurt you."

She shrugs, "It was just a slap."

"Just a..."

She reaches for my hand as the doctor inspects her and asks her to open her mouth.

"No cuts," he says, under his breath.

"No, it wasn't a punch. I'm okay."

The doctor looks from her to me, and politely excuses himself. Justin approaches us as he glances over to where Jason sits beside Bernie, holding her hand. "The police want to talk to you, Drew."

"What'd they ask you?"

"What we were doing there. They're not surprised we fucked the guys up. Bernie's head is enough to show them the girls were in trouble, that we did what we had to."

Drew and I head out to talk with them. Neither of us is looking forward to this. We haven't agreed on what to say. She glances to me with a look that says she's worried. I take her hand and approach two members of the Atlanta P.D. Both men who have seen it all. One black, one white. Their hands are on their belts as they turn to face us.

Drew explains her side of what went down as the corridor buzzes with nurses and doctors moving quickly around the four of us, from one patient to the next.

When asked if there's anything she's leaving out, Drew stares at the floor for a long moment. "Yes, my friend has been hiding that she's a prostitute."

The policemen look at each other then glance from me back to Drew. "You know this for a fact?"

"Yes," Drew sighs. "I used to live with her. I didn't

know the men who came by were paying her. I just thought she was addicted to the drugs and they were giving her some." She sees their narrowing eyes and quickly adds, "I've known her since we were little. I know what you're thinking, cocaine is illegal, but I'm sorry to say a lot of people are doing illegal things and not ratting their friends out about it."

This reality, and honesty, relaxes the policemen. I put my hand on Drew's lower back for support, to let her know I'm here.

She clarifies, "And I didn't know she was selling her body until today," as if that would have made her second-think turning a blind eye.

"This isn't the first time," I tell them as Drew looks up at me. "My brother used to date Bernie and he knew about it for a long while. He used to try to protect her. She's an addict. She can't stop herself."

Drew frowns from me to the cops as they inform her, "You know we have to arrest her now."

"Yes, I do," she quietly says. "Thank you."

"You're going to have to submit to drug testing, too."

"Of course. That's fine. I'm clean. Can I go see her now?"

They nod like they're watching her.

Drew sighs as we head back to the hospital room where Justin is waiting just outside the door. "I could hear all that."

"Drew's hoping this will be what gets Bernie sober."

She looks up at me, a little surprised I caught on. "Yes," she says, taking my hand and leaning into me.

Kissing the top of her head, I ask Justin, "How's he doing?"

"Who knows? She's his Kryptonite. You remember," mutters Justin as he cuts a glance into the cold white room. "This is going to take some time. I'll get us some food. Hang on."

He walks over to the policemen and with his usual ability to charm people, has them laughing within seconds. I couldn't hear what he whispered, but he raises his voice to ask, "So you don't mind if I bring us all back some pizzas?"

"Nah." "That's fine."

He comes strolling up to us with a big smile.

"I'll go with you," I tell him, and give Drew a kiss. "I'll be back soon. I know you want to stay with her."

She nods and touches my cheek. "Thank you, Jake. I know you don't like her."

"That doesn't matter right now."

She nods and squeezes my hand before I head off with my brother. When we're out of earshot, I tell him, "I hope Bernie stays behind bars forever."

"No fucking joke, man," he grumbles. "The girl is dangerous."

"*H*ome has never felt so good," I sigh, as we take off our shoes. I'm absolutely exhausted. "Being tested for drugs makes you feel like a criminal!"

Jake reaches over, locks the deadbolt, and smiles, "C'mere you crook."

I step into his embrace and guiltily melt into him. He's been so good to me tonight. "I feel terrible you had to go through all of this for me."

"Hey hey hey. Stop that." He lifts my chin, eyes full of feeling. "If you didn't have me to call, you know what would have happened? I'm just glad I came back in time. If I was still in Denver...I'd be going to jail for finding those motherfuckers and tearing their dicks off with my bare hands."

I shudder and burrow into his rock-solid body, loving how safe he makes me feel. He takes my hand

and leads me to his room. "You've never been in here before, have you?"

Swallowing, I lie, "No. I wanted to peek when you were away, but it would have been too hard, so I didn't."

"Well, I looked in your room once."

I gasp and meet his smiling eyes. "You did!?"

He chuckles, "Yeah, I guess I was curious. You kept fucking running away and I didn't know anything about you."

I can't believe he did that! I'm really having a hard time picturing it. And now that I said I didn't go into his, can I take it back? "What did you find? I don't have a journal so it must have been very boring."

"Nope. Not boring," he smirks, leading me to his bed. "I know you've been through a lot, so let's just sleep together here tonight." Struggling to decide if I want to confess I'd stared at this bed in agony as I pictured him here with Bernie, I decide he's right, tonight was overwhelming. That's probably why I lied just now—to avoid talking about Bernie anymore. Neither of us wants to.

Jake starts undressing me, fingers pausing at my missing button. His jaw flexes in anger as he locks eyes with me.

"What'd you find in my room?" I smile, guiding him to a nicer subject.

From the way he blinks, it's hard for him to let his protective anger go. His voice is thick with the struggle.

"The books you were studying. 7 Habits of Highly Successful People, and all those."

Pulling my shirt off, he inspects me for bruises. "He didn't touch me there, Jake. I promise I'd tell you."

"Even if you know I'd want to kill him?"

"Even then. I won't lie again." *And I'll tell you I was in your room later. But that was my last lie, I promise.* "I saw how mad you were when the doctor checked my face."

Jake frowns before he kisses my collarbone, unsnapping my bra and freeing me from it. He glances to my naked breasts and dips to kiss the pillowy flesh just above my right nipple. "I wish you'd told me you were going over there before you left."

I'm trying to be light as I smile, "You were sleeping. You were passed out! Snoring!"

Jake's eyes are stubborn, cloudy with the wish to go back in time. "I could have gone with you."

I whisper, "I'm sorry," meaning it more than he knows. He pulls off his shirt and undoes his jeans, tugging them down and stepping out of them. His socks get yanked off, then my jeans, panties and socks.

Like a tamed beast, he crawls onto his bed to lie with me on top of the covers. It's very humid out tonight, and our body heat will be more than enough to keep us warm.

"Drew?" he rasps, coming up on his elbow to see me better.

Tracing his chest muscles lovingly I murmur, "Mmm?"

He pauses a beat and says, "I don't want to lose you."

My fingertips stop where they are, and I meet his eyes, searching them, finding only sincerity staring back at me. "I don't want to be lost."

Jake gives me the slowest, most sensual kiss of my life, one that makes me believe he might love me. My leg instinctively wraps around him. Caught up in the moment, he rolls on top of me as our tongues touch. Our hands explore each others bodies with tender learning. Places I normally never think much of, become erogenous zones.

His naked erection grows urgent against my pelvis, but Jake makes no move to do anything about it. After we kiss for a long while, I reach to touch it. He groans as my fingers wrap around his hardened length and hold.

"Baby, we don't have to."

"I want to. I'm okay, really I am. I need you." I hold his look to explain what I mean, "*You* want to touch me for the right reasons, Jake."

He closes his eyes, taking that in, and kisses me. My lungs expand with my heart. The kiss awakens us as our mouths mold each other's. We take our sweet time, find this new way for us to make love. Rough can wait another day.

There's no hurry.

We have each other now.

Jake moves my legs a little and slowly starts to enter me while looking into my eyes to make sure I'm okay.

It's a new feeling, being with a man like him. He cares and shows it in ways that matter to me. Maybe I'm wrong but I think all women want to be made love to by someone who cares this much and puts hesitation on hold in order to show it.

I watch the pleasure transform his features as he ever-so-slowly presses into my wet folds. We moan together, and Jake pushes all his weight onto me, crushing me in the most delicious way, like he wants me to know from now on he will be my shield.

I tilt my chin and he kisses open, waiting lips. Our fingers entwine as my legs hook around him, and we start to rock like this with him undulating slowly, electricity lighting us up from the inside.

Jake growls in my ear, "I could do this forever."

I squeeze his hands, and his hips with my legs, arching up as he maintains a slow and steady rhythm. The ache becomes so desperate that I cry out, wincing against the urge for release. Jake starts moving faster. I whimper his name as my orgasm tiptoes into me, getting an inch closer with each slow thrust.

We wrap our arms around each other and he brings me up onto his lap, expertly fucking me in this new position. I try to hold on, but I feel overwhelmed by all of this. "Hold me up," I murmur, and his arms lock around my body.

He groans long and low as my pussy tightens and clenches. "You're cumming... I can feel it." He starts fucking me harder, abandoning himself to his own climax.

His sends mine deeper, and I start to cry from sheer happiness. He smashes our lips together, kisses me as his cum shoots into me again and again.

"Fuck, baby," he growls, kisses me and smirks, "I'm going to marry you."

"Wait now," I gasp, blinking quickly. "I'm still married."

He stares back at me, speechless. We both start laughing like complete idiots.

"Jesus," he groans.

"I know. I'm a slut."

Rolling his eyes he grins, "Yeah, but you're my slut," kissing my tears away. "Time to get those papers signed."

*W*earing nothing but a smile, I toss pancakes high in the air. "We could make your room an office."

Drew smiles as I catch them. "You're very good at that." She's naked, too, leaning against our kitchen island with only half of her orange juice left. "I think I should keep my bedroom."

My eyebrow shoots up. "Why?"

"Because this might not work out."

Chuckling I nod, "Yeah, the past week has been hell."

"A week is not forever, Jake."

Lowering the heat on the stove, I throw her a smirk. "You sound like a teacher."

She holds back a smile, pretending to be irritated. "I'm not trying to teach you. These are just facts."

Turning the pan, I shake golden brown pancakes onto a plate. Behind it is the maple syrup I heated up, plus sliced strawberries and powdered sugar. As I construct my masterpiece for us to share, I explain, "What you don't seem to get is how well I know myself. Not sure if you noticed, roomie, but—"

She laughs, "Oh, I noticed!"

"—I was brought up to be my own man. My brothers, the same. It's easy to call us *cocky* because of our last name. What baffles me is that they say it like it's a bad thing—as if demeaning yourself, diminishing your worth, is better than owning it. That's some backwards thinking, isn't it? Does that make any kind of sense to you? Why is it better to put yourself down?" I glance to her before I return to strawberry overload, shaking my head. "People want to control you by your insecurities. Fuck that."

Drew whispers, "Fuck that."

Picking up our single plate, I open the utensil drawer and snatch out two forks, closing it with my hip. "What people don't realize is that ever since birth my brothers and I were taught that we were put on this planet for a reason. *Everyone is.* Being insecure is a waste of our fucking time. We could be spending that being who we were meant to be, which by nature would help the rest of us grow, right? A rising tide lifts all boats." Drew is staring at me like she can't believe this profound thinking is coming from me. She has a lot to learn. Jett isn't the only surprising Cocker Brother. I haven't paid my own way all these years because I'm a slouch. As we dig in, I shrug, "And sure, everyone has fears. That's part of the game of life. It's overcoming them, that's how you win."

Syrup threatens to drip from her fork as Drew brings a heaping portion to her mouth. She takes a bite, blue eyes closing with a long, "Mmmm."

"You like it?"

"I guess I'm never cooking."

"Dream on."

With her mouthful, she laughs, and chews like this is the best thing she's ever had. After the night we had, I gave her an appetite. It's only fair I give her nourishment, too. Especially because I'm not done fucking her senseless.

As she scoops up a wandering strawberry, Drew's eyes cloud over. "Did I tell you my father is a pastor?"

My head cocks to the side. "Nope."

"He is."

"I can't wait to meet him."

She stares at me, then smiles, "Me too."

Through a mouthful I ask, "He won't approve?"

"I didn't say that!"

"Yeah, you did."

Poking at the pancakes, she thinks about it. "He doesn't approve of much. I guess he worries about me."

Snorting, I turn to our refrigerator for more juice. "If I had a daughter *and* she was my only kid, you better believe I'd worry. Want more?"

"Yes, please."

Pouring into our empty glasses I imagine that scenario. Convinced, I nod, "Yep, I'd be a tyrant, no doubt. Hell, if I had a little girl, she'd stay single until I was dead!"

Drew laughs, "You'd better not have any girls, then."

Our eyes lock and we're both picturing the same thing—us having kids. I know she wants them, from her story about her husband, and the announcement the first time we had sex.

I never expected my reaction to that.

But if anyone asked me if I wanted a family, I'd have said, *of course. A big one. Later.*

Then Drew showed up.

This woman changed my life and there's no way I want the old one back. Am I ready for a family? Not sure. Especially since there's one thing standing in my way.

*M*y brother did me a favor. Justin's connections are growing into a larger net of influence. His desire to become a Senator someday has made him a lot of friends.

I couldn't ask Dad for this one.

Justin was happy to help out.

Especially since he's been on edge with Jason watching over Bernie's release from jail, her admittance into a rehab clinic. I asked about it and Justin was tight-lipped. So I pushed the subject and he lost his temper with me, saying, "There's no fucking way he's falling under her spell under my watch!"

If he were so sure, he wouldn't be so pissed.

When I checked in on Jason, he claimed detachment. But there was something in his voice...

First problems first.

Drew.

My first love.

I'm hoping, my only.

Drew has been over to our parents' house again, for my welcome back dinner last weekend.

Aunt Anna, Uncle Dave and my cousins got to meet her. Everyone is surprised I have a girlfriend, but they all like her. I want to keep it that way.

Nobody except for my brothers—and maybe Uncle Don—knows Drew is married. We live in the south, and marriage is for good. With how protective my family is, well, I can't imagine what Mom and Dad would say.

Drew doesn't deserve judgment for the failure of her first go-round.

And she ain't gonna be fuckin' married for long.

Not to him anyway.

I have plans of my own.

"I'm sorry, but I don't have you on the schedule," the shorthaired receptionist explains as she scratches her face at the computer screen.

"Allergy?" I ask.

She glances to me, confusion quickly replaced by awareness of what she was doing. She drops her hand. "Oh, yeah. I'm allergic to dairy, but I love ice cream, soooo..."

"Oh, that sucks. But nothing better than mint chocolate chip." This earns me the first smile she's given since I walked in. She's a dike, so my charms have fallen flat. I don't have the people-skills of Justin, much as I hate to admit it. Bonding over allergy-talk is my fallback option. "Listen, I'm not on the list, but we go

way back, so I'll just go in and say hey. Won't be long."
She's about to object when I just go for it. "Thanks!" I
call over my shoulder.

Her mouth is open as she watches me, but I get in
without her argument.

His argument is waiting for me inside.

The guy from the photo on Drew's shelf looks up
as I walk into his office. It's a boring-ass room, that's all
that can be said of it.

I walk over and pick up the photo on his desk that's
facing him, so I can see it. It's not of Drew.

"Excuse me! Who're you?!"

I slam the photo down. "I'm your wife's boyfriend."

Edward Charles gapes, sizing me up, not happy
with what's standing in front of him. I can tell the
image of me between Drew's legs is flashing across his
mind. This dude's best years were in high school.

Not mine.

Mine are still coming.

Now that I met her.

"How *old* are you?"

"Old enough to know a good thing when I find it.
Here." I toss the manila envelope onto the desk. I stole
this from Drew's room earlier, happy to see this fuck-
head's photo wasn't on display there anymore.

"What's this?" He opens it and pulls out divorce
papers.

"She's giving you the house and you're giving her
whatever amount she asked for in return."

"I made the money in..."

"Listen, you fuck!" I storm around the desk and lift him off his chair. "You told her not to work so she could be a mother and then you had your fucking girly-tubes tied without letting her in on it. Fucking her how many years while she's hoping ONE TIME would produce what she'd been promised. From my face, does it look like I have patience with that kind of betrayal? So Edward, YOU REALLY WANNA GO THERE WITH ME?"

He blinks, shakes his head. I drop him into his seat, and lean in to poke his chest with my fist. "My family goes waaaaaaaaay back here in Georgia. Our ties run deep. This little company you've built for yourself? You want your customers to keep coming, right?"

"Are you threatening me?"

"Are you an idiot? *The answer is yes.* You want to test me? Because we can do this two ways. You can go crying to whoever you think would help you, *and lose everything,* or you can sign the divorce papers, give Drew her due, and go about your business with your pretty new lady and her about-to-pop belly." I cross my arms. "That second one sounds like a better option, doesn't it?"

"If I sign, this is over and you'll leave us alone?"

"You sign that right now? You'll never see me again."

Edward's hands shake as he reaches for the papers and a pen. Glancing from me to them, he signs in all the places highlighted for his signature.

"You're a fucking moron, you know that?" I mutter.

"What?! Wait, did you put something in there that screws me over and I just signed it?!!"

"No, twat, you're a moron because you walked away from a woman like Drew. Fucking idiot." I grab the official papers, shoving them in the envelope as I head out.

He calls after me with disgust, "You're just a child!"

I stop at his door and smirk at him. "I'm a man, Edward. Unlike you, you snake. Have a great fuckin' day."

Outside, the receptionist is standing at her desk, her eyes on me as I approach.

She heard everything.

I slow down, considering how to handle this.

I shouldn't have yelled.

I didn't want a witness.

She whispers, so her boss can't hear her, "Tell Drew I said, *well done!*" Pausing, I take this in. Off my expression, she explains in the same low volume, "I always loved her. Such a nice person. Didn't deserve what happened to her."

I walk up, shake the woman's hand. "What's your name?"

"Janet."

"I'll tell her. Thanks, Janet."

Strolling into sunshine with a grin on my face, I pull out my excited phone.

Drew answers on the first ring, "Hey, I'm in the

middle of something. When are you leaving the job site and coming back here?"

"I'm not at the job site."

"What? I thought you said —"

"—I'm in Dublin, Georgia."

"Why are you in...Jake! What did you do?"

I laugh and tell her, "Claimed what's yours for you, baby. And I needed to pave the way for what we talked about last night."

She pauses in shock. Her voice lowers. "We were in the heat of the moment, Jake. It's too soon to talk about marriage. And what do you mean, you claimed what's mine?"

"Your divorce papers are signed. Oh, and Janet says hello."

"JAKE!!!"

She starts swearing, which always amuses me. I hang up on her, laughing to myself as I slide into the driver's seat, shut the door and blast some old-school Rolling Stones for my ride home, singin' along as best I can.

I ignore all of the insistent calls from her. She can show me how mad she is when I get her naked tonight. Oh man, is there gonna be some sweet fuckin' this evenin'! Gonna have claw marks on me for days.

I can't wait to get home. But that's me every day now. Home really is where the heart is. Drew has changed my life. Never thought I'd be this happy with one woman, but then again I don't think I'd ever really *known* myself until I became the man she could love. Nurturing her, loving her, supporting her as she continues her studies and joins the 'city life' that still inspires wonder in her eyes...all these things make me feel like I have something to offer the world. She's my world. And someday soon I'm going to make her a mother.

The mother of *my* children.

I can't wait to get home...

FOUR YEARS LATER

"*D*rew honey, give me a hand with this chili. Just turn it over a bunch while I say hello to my favorite person in the whole world!"

I gently kiss my daughter's brown, wispy baby-hair before handing little Emma to her grandmother. "I don't know, Nancy. This is a big responsibility," I tease, picking up the ladle she set down.

While cooing into Emma's ear and bouncing her, Nancy receives a kiss on her own cheek from my husband. She chides him, "Jake, this little girl makes me forgive you for being late today, but just barely."

"I know, I'm sorry. We were busy."

He winks at me and I shake my head behind her back, silently warning him to stop being so damned obvious. She doesn't need to know we were late because Emma took an unexpected nap that inspired my horny man to steal me into the hallway for a good hard fucking. That led to *another* shower. Which further led to us arriving after everyone else, and my forgetting the potatoes he made.

"What's this?!" Jason calls out as he finds me with the chili. "Mom! You never let me touch that! How come Drew gets to?! You only ever ask me to carry it!"

"Give me a grandchild, Jason Cocker, and that chili is all yours," she wickedly smiles. "Huh, Emma, don't you need a cousin from your Uncle Jason, huh?"

"I'm workin' on it, Mom." Jason rolls his eyes and greets me with a kiss on my cheek. "Hey sis."

"Hi Jason."

He bear hugs Jake. "Good to see you. Jax is out back."

"What about Justin?"

"Still on the road shmoozing with political mucky-mucks." Jason touches Emma's head with love as her big brown eyes soak him in. "Like this little beauty right here." He kisses her forehead while Nancy holds her out so he can. Emma's pudgy arms flail like crazy all of a sudden. She's only fourteen months, curious and full of energy. Enraptured, Jason asks the room, "Does this mean I should go into politics? She loves me!"

His ears perk to the sound of his wife calling for him, and he runs outside.

Jake chuckles, and comes up behind me, arms sliding around my body. He lays his head on my shoulder to survey slow turns of the family's infamous chili addiction. "Hi sexy."

"Jaxson's waiting for you, baby."

He whispers in my ear, "Let him wait," giving it a single lick. I touch his arm, wrapped around my middle, and smile, relaxing into his strength.

Four years and we're still happy. There've been a few bumps, like when we told his parents about Edward. Nancy had hoped the first son to marry would do so in a more traditional circumstance. She made it very clear neither she nor Michael believe in divorce. Jake got pretty angry, explained maybe a little too much of my situation, all private details included. That embarrassed me, but it turned out that he was right in doing so. It gave her deep compassion for me, and we grew quite close.

The only real problems Jake and I have had, involved other people. On our own, we balance each other out extremely well. He's gregarious where I'm shy. I'm grounded, where he flies off the handle at every passionate whim.

We spent a couple years with just us before we made the choice to grow our family. I needed those years alone with him, despite how much I'd always wanted children. Jake thought we'd launch right in. He was surprised when I paused that plan.

"Well, what the hell?!" Jeremy shouts as he strolls into the kitchen from the backyard porch. "Come out and say hello to everyone!"

Jake yells out, and runs over to pick his younger brother up. "You're back early!"

Jeremy laughs, "Nah!" looking at Nancy.

My husband and I both look over at her, reading her sneaky face as he gasps, "Mom!"

"Jake, I wanted it to be a surprise! Now don't you look at me like that."

"Give me back my daughter, you liar." He rushes over to dramatically remove Emma from Nancy's arms as she profusely objects. Ignoring her, he murmurs, "Hello Baby Love, you want to be with your daddy, don't you?" Of course Emma grins like wild at him. "See? She wants to be with me, Mom, sorry."

"You're just rude!" Nancy cries out. "Give me back that baby! I wanted Jeremy's coming home to be a surprise so I said the wrong date. You do that to me all the time!"

My mother runs in. "Did I hear Emma is here?!"

"Hi Momma," I smile. "Good to see you, too."

She rolls her eyes and grabs my daughter. "Jake, give me this little preciousness. Just for a little while, because I'm beating your father at cribbage, Drew!"

With heavy sarcasm I say, "Well, that's a first," because she always beats him.

"Oh stop! Emma, aren't you the most beautiful little girl in the whole world?" Emma smiles at Momma a little shyly. She doesn't get to see them as much since they still live in Dublin. "She's bigger, Jake, isn't she?"

"Well, of course she's bigger," Nancy answers for him, chomping at the bit to hold Emma again. "Let me see her!"

"Now honey," Michael Cocker laughs, walking

inside with the sun at his broad shoulders. "You've got another one outside waiting for you to dote all over him."

Nancy glowers like it's a conspiracy, gives up and hurriedly checks the chili before rushing outside, calling behind her, "Tell Jeremy and Jason to bring that chili out in two more minutes!"

Jeremy walks up to me, arms out. "Drew!"

"You look so tan, Jeremy!" I smile, giving him a big hug. "It's been too long since I've seen you."

"You'll be seeing a lot more of me from now on."

"I wish we could say the same about Jerald," the Congressman mutters.

Jeremy and I exchange a subtle look while my husband says, "It's Jett now, Dad. When are you gonna give that up?"

"Never," he grumbles, vanishing outside.

And that's probably why you won't see Jett.

I filled my momma in years ago about the trouble they have. She gives me a meaningful look as she walks Emma to me. "Well, now, that's just gotta stop!"

"Not now, Momma."

"I'm just sayin' it's a shame. Oh well. People can be very stubborn." She smiles at Emma and touches her cheek as I bounce her on my hip. "Your father's waitin' for you to say hello."

"I'm comin' now."

Jake walks over to me with his mind on his father and Jett. I know that expression very well by now.

"You okay?"

"Yeah," he mutters, then breaks out of the mood, pointing to Jeremy, "Now that this one's staying for good." They exchange a smile before Jake spins around with a sneaky look on his handsome face. "I'll get the chili. It'll irritate Mom."

Jeremy starts laughing.

Sure enough, as Jake appears with it and not using any help—it's a huge pot—she spots him from all the way down in the yard. "I said for Jeremy and Jason to grab that!"

"Too bad, Mom!"

"Don't drop it!"

He shoots me a look. "She still thinks I'm twelve."

"Aren't you?" I mutter.

"Very funny, babe. Hilarious."

*L*ater that night, we watch Emma sleeping, and he stands behind me like he did when I was turning the chili. His head is on my shoulder again and we're both smiling at the gentle rise and fall of her tiny chest. "I love how she sleeps with her mouth open like that," he whispers.

"She got that from you," I whisper back.

"No, I don't sleep like that."

"I'm waiting for her to start snoring like you, too."

He lightly spanks my butt and I turn my head to receive a kiss. "Baby, I have something I need to tell you."

Dark eyebrows shoot up, and he motions for us to leave the baby's room.

This place is my pride and joy, the first thing I decorated when we bought this home a year ago, right after she was born.

Emma would lie in her little carrier next to me while I picked out colors and decals for her walls. I showed them to her and asked which she loved the most, laughing and calling out to my husband that our daughter apparently has a thing for pale yellow.

"Look at this!" I told him as he rushed into the room. "Emma, you like this color?" I held up green and she just stared at it. "How about pink?" More curious staring. I showed him the yellow swatch first and then held it in front of Emma. "What about...oh you like that one, huh!?" She squirmed, smiling and reaching for it.

"Wow!" he grinned, kneeling down beside her. Brown eyes just like her daddy's flitted over to take him in. "You like yellow, huh Emma?" I watched him lean down and kiss her head, with so much love filling my heart.

Everything about this room is special to me.

The furniture was mostly gifted from our families when they found out we were pregnant and would be providing the first grandchild. Nancy went nuts with gifts. We donated some of them to a local shelter, but won't tell her that. Can't blame her for getting that excited—it had been a long time since she'd had a baby in her life. And this would be the first girl for her, even if she had to wait for a grandchild to get one.

We painted the room ourselves, too, while our Emma watched, so it really was a family effort. This is something I'll tell her a million times when she's old enough to remember.

Jake leads me into a much larger kitchen than the one we shared at the apartment where he threw microwave popcorn away after I narrowly escaped his first seduction. "Did something happen today while I wasn't looking?"

"No, my daddy got along with yours this time."

Jake nods. "Well, that's a relief."

"It's something else, baby. It has to do with work."

"Did Uncle Don not give you that raise?"

"Um...no, he did. But the thing is, I might have to turn it down." My heart is picking up speed now. I can see I'm worrying Jake, but I'm a little nervous about what I want to propose to him. "There's something I want to do that is going to sound out of character, but hear me out."

Jake shoves his hands into his pockets, classic Cocker male sign of discomfort. They have no idea this gives them away every time. He leans against the counter, face calm. "Spill it."

I pause for courage. "I want to quit working for a while."

Jake blinks at me and cocks his head like he didn't hear me right. "Say that again? Why?"

"I want to go to college. Online college and it's hard to take care of Emma—"

"—Oh, well that makes sense, Drew," he exhales,

and frees his hands, walking to me. "Why are you so nervous?"

"You didn't let me finish," I smile.

Jake takes my fingers, entwining them with his. "Well, now's your chance. Hurry up, because I'm about to interrupt you again, and tell you that college sounds great. You don't have to go online, though. If you want to go to regular classes, Mom would love to watch Emma."

"No, I want to stay home with Emma. And I want to be here for the new baby, too."

He stares at me, blinks, "New baby?"

"Uh huh," I smile, leaning in to watch his face change.

"There's a new baby?"

"In about...six months...yup."

My husband's eyes go as big as my heart. He hollers and lifts me, kissing me hard before he spins me around. "Holy hell, Drew! Why didn't you tell me before the BBQ? We could have announced it!"

"I was plannin' on it, but then your mom called me so excited about Jeremy, and made me promise not to tell you he was home. So I realized he should be the big surprise today. He earned that."

Jake's watching me explain with a look of total love on his face. "Drew, sometimes I think I don't deserve you."

"You don't."

I yelp as he yanks my new sundress up and buries his face in my stomach.

"Who's in there? Eve? Erika? Hmmm? What's your name?"

Slipping my fingers in his hair and admiring my beautiful wedding ring, I quietly confess, "I'm hoping it's *Ethan,* honey."

Jake looks up at me. "I wasn't even thinking it might be a boy." Off my tiny shrug, he says from down there, "I'm fine with either," as he slips my panties down.

"Jake, what are you doing?"

"I love fucking you when you're pregnant," he murmurs into my inner thigh as he spreads my legs. "You're so horny it's insane."

I moan under his kisses, "Well, that part hasn't begun yet. That's later when I'm huge and unattractive. It's God's irony."

Ignoring my 'unattractive' comment, Jake murmurs, "Let's jump-start it."

My panties are suddenly gone and my husband has buried his face in my pussy. He breathes me in and groans. I hold onto the counter for a good long while. Jake slowly licks me until I'm begging for his cock, nice and quietly so we don't wake Emma.

He lifts me onto the countertop, turns on the sink and lets cold water run over his hands. I gasp as he slides those fingers over my nipples right before unzipping his fly. Our mouths latch together and move with a hunger we have come to love in each other. We are sexually perfectly suited. We bicker about all kinds of stupid stuff, as all couples do, but all Jake has to do is motion to his crotch and the tension vanishes into laughter.

Today, I watched him with his family—now my own—and realized once more that Edward really did do me a favor when he left me for that woman. I have no idea what happened to them. I don't even care, because my life today is so full.

I'm not the vengeful type, but they say the best way to get back at someone who hurt you is live a happy life.

Jake likes to remind me that I almost didn't date him because he was younger than me. I tell him, *I still want out.* It drives him crazy when I say that, because I keep my face very somber when I tease him about it, but we both know I'm not going anywhere.

My legs wrap around his narrow hips as he moves to penetrate. "What are you waitin' for?" I whisper with a challenge in my eyes. He groans as the tip begs for admission into my body. I moan into his ear with each welcome inch. Letting our pleasure guide us, we move slowly. As our mouths find each other, lock and mold, everything heats up. Our passion has grown so much deeper since we said, '*I do.*'

Jake growls and stops kissing me so he can watch me cum in his arms. He pounds me with swift, hard strokes as I go over the edge, whimpering his name. I want to cry out, but I can't with the baby sleeping in the other room.

"Fuck, *Drew Cocker,* you're cumming *so* hard. I can feel you dripping down my cock!" He groans as his head falls back, neck pulsing. Hot juices explode into me, and I shiver with tingles, my arms around him as we lock tongues. Thick pulses take their sweet time rippling through our bodies as we move, enjoying the moment.

He gasps and shakes his head like he's lost the ability to think straight. "Drew?"

Kissing his stubble all the way to his ear, I whisper, "Mmm?"

"I will be happy with a girl, but...I hope this is Ethan, honey. Emma needs a brother to watch over her."

My arms tighten around him, and I watch sweat beading at his temple. "I love you, Jake."

Relaxing into me, he murmurs, "I love you, too, baby."

*S*ix months and fourteen days later, Ethan *Jett* Cocker will take his first breath to join a growing family. Not just with me and Drew and Emma, but our entire Cocker family who will love him more than he can handle, and sometimes drive him bat-shit crazy, too. Little do we know he will pay us back for that when he grows up and is smarter than the lot of us.

Cockers...we always watch over our own, protect, love, fight, forgive—united. We're not perfect, but that's what being *human* is all about. I just want a wild ride, and love is that for me.

THE END.

"*Cocker Brothers*" *is written in chronological order, stories intertwining in titillating ways. Jake is the first of six brothers, each with their own exciting and steamy novels.*

Then the wild next generation takes over your favorite Cocker Family traditions.

*Jett Cocker is next as his club fights for the innocent, then **Jaxson's Second Chance love story**, the twins **Jason & Justin** fighting hard against falling in love, and finally **Jeremy** needs to find his way back home.*

If you'd like to jump to the grown up children of Jake and Drew — Ethan, Emma, and Eric's books — they are available now, too!

(In chronological order, not the order of their ages: **Cocky Genius, Cocky Love,** *and* **Cocky Quarterback***)*

COCKER BROTHERS SERIES

"The Cocker series is the best roller coaster reading experience available on Amazon." - USMCWife1978

(FOR HOW THE SERIES WORKS, SCROLL/TURN THE PAGE.)

COCKER FAMILY EXTRAS

ON MY WEBSITE...
www.AuthorFaleenaHopkins.com
Free Bonus Scenes
Merchandise Benefitting Charity
Signed Paperbacks
Bookmarks & Stickers
Family Tree to help keep you track

SPOTIFY — SERIES PLAYLISTS
*Made by the fabulous blogger "Belle Reader" — a labor
of love for which I'm eternally grateful.*

ABOUT THE AUTHOR

Previously a stand-up comic for 5 years when she lived in Los Angeles, Faleena Hopkins now performs on 2 improv-comedy teams in NYC where she moved in 2017. In between those two cities, she spent a year and a half acting and writing in Atlanta, Georgia, where *Cocker Brothers* was born. Her directorial debut, a ghost love story feature film, *Just One More Kiss,* launches in 2019. You can find the trailer and know when it releases at: MorningDovePictures.com
She plans on writing the Cocker Brothers series until all the cousins get their own forever loves, and maybe longer. We shall see!

You can see her acting/filmmaking work on IMDB.com